ALSO BY NEIL JORDAN

NIGHT IN TUNISIA

THE PAST

THE DREAM OF A BEAST

THE CRYING GAME (SCREENPLAY)

NIGHTLINES

NIGHTLINES

NEIL JORDAN

RANDOM HOUSE NEW YORK

All rights reserved under International and Pan-American Copyright
Conventions. Published in the United States by Random House, Inc.,
New York.

This work was originally published in Great Britain by Chatto &
Windus Ltd., London, in 1994 as *Sunrise with Sea Monster*.

Library of Congress Cataloging-in-Publication Data
Jordan, Neil.
Nightlines / Neil Jordan.
p.   cm.
ISBN 0–679–44439–4 (alk. paper)
I. Title.
PR6060.06255N54   1995
823'.914—dc20   95–16076

Manufactured in the United States of America on acid-free paper
24689753
First U.S. Edition

BOOK DESIGN BY LILLY LANGOTSKY

FOR BRENDA

NOTE ON HISTORICAL BACKGROUND

Ireland was neutral during the Second World War, a policy that led to much that was sinister, much that was ridiculous. The country had achieved independence from Britain, but at a cost. The War of Independence (1918–21) had led to a treaty with Britain that was rejected by the more radical factions within the Irish Republican Army. These divisions led to a civil war, where those for and against the treaty fought with a savagery that surpassed that of the War of Independence itself. Eamon De Valera led the anti-treaty faction, Liam Cosgrave the pro-treaty government. Normal politics resumed when the Civil War exhausted itself, and in 1932 Eamon De Valera won a majority and was elected Taoiseach (prime minister). He was to dominate the politics of Ireland for the next forty years. His former comrades in the IRA who disagreed with any accommodation with the treaty were then outlawed and suppressed. As the Second World War drew closer, the IRA itself split into factions that mirrored the divisions in Europe. One faction supported the fight against fascism, particularly in Spain. The other regarded England's enemy as its natural ally and was thus drawn into support for Nazi Germany.

De Valera pursued his policy of neutrality during the Second World War with extraordinary rigor, ruthlessly proscribing the splintered remnants of the IRA, censoring the press, and effectively sealing off the Irish Republic from any contact with events in Europe.

For further information, see the Glossary on p. 191.

NIGHTLINES

I

They file out with the first light and let us stand there for an hour or two. The light will change, we know, from dim silver to a blinding white during our stasis and, for the few minutes of what they properly call dawn, the giant poster of the Virgin will have a sky of ribboned magenta behind it. Almost a halo, of the quite conventional kind, which adorns as an afterthought the poster of the Spaniard to her left and the Italian to her right. Though their shared glory will take some time to arrive. Both Mussolini and Franco flap against their wooden supports in the wind the heatening sun drives before it, wearing similar hats, painted with the same monumental rigidity, flicking with each thwack, as if mildly epileptic. She smiles in between, moved only by the same occasional twitch, a sad smile on her face, a rigid smile, a monumental one but not

3

too different really from the smiles on the statues back home.

Behind her, on the wooden box-towers, the Moroccans stand, half sleeping in their uniforms, one of them banging the nails of the boards that hold him. He doesn't care for the light changing behind him, maybe because he has to stand all day. I can imagine anything behind those monastery walls, but nothing that would generate a flicker of interest from his eyes. We care, since we know that the nauseous riot of colour behind her is only there to signal the procession out of the barred doors, the priest coming last behind his peasant altar-boys, their vestments grubby and white, barely concealing their khaki uniforms.

The Spaniards to one side, feet swollen under knots of rags, resigned already to what they know will face them. The dark stains on the monastery wall, twenty yards from the Virgin's left hand, catch the eye only in so far as every eye tries to avoid them. The Jewish kid from Turin, his large eyes forever regretting whatever immoderation drove him here. And the rest of us stand bound by a common tough thread. Not being our fight, it could well not be our execution, a thought that plays with a sly unwitting smile behind each face, the way a child who hears of death for the first time can but laugh, then suppresses it with the most appropriate demeanour. So we stand there, tough, resilient and apparently bored.

I remember my father, and what got me here. We would lay nightlines, in our rare moments of tranquillity, on the beach below the terrace where our house was. Thin strings of gut between two metal rods strung intermittently with hooks, much like the barbed wire that joins the box-towers, on one of which the Moroccan still bangs with his rifle-butt. We would jam them in the hard sand at low tide; evening was always best, when all the water had retreated and the low light hit the ridges of the scalloped sand. A mackerel sky behind us, more tranquil than the one now forming behind the Virgin's head. The lines pulled taut, each hook neatly tied, his trousers rolled around his calves, bare feet against the ridged sand. A shovel, and a rapid succession of holes dug, around each ragworm cast. There were rags and lugs, I remember, the one all arms like a centipede, the other like a bulbous eel, both adequate for the task in hand. Which was to walk back to where the lines were strung, shoes in one hand, squirming mass of worms in the other, feet splaying sideways over the ridges of sand, and skewer a worm on to each waiting hook. By which time the sun was almost gone and the rags and lugs would swing gently squirming, dark against the dying light. We would turn without a word after watching for a while as if words would have fractured the moment's—peace, I would have said, but that would have implied a continuity of such moments between us, which there wasn't. Respite would be truer, respite from the many gradations of awkward speech, and more awkward silences. Whatever the word, we both knew this moment and would let nothing broach it, would walk back along the ribbed sand, my feet splayed to save them discomfort, his firm, set flat across the scallops, bigger, harder, infinitely older. Shoes in one hand, shovel in the other.

The next morning there would be the catch, of course, when the tide went out. A couple of plaice, a salmon bass, a dogfish, swinging between the lines, which would be bent with the weight, silver against the silver tide. We would walk out and could talk now; I being the kid would run towards them, he being the father would identify each in that didactic way of his. I'd walk towards him, my arms full of poles, wet fish and catgut. The reaping was never as rich as the sowing, somehow. I knew that then and would connect that paradox with speech. The words, the sunlight, maybe the fact that the tide had come in. In the house behind us she would already be being lifted from her bed for Sunday dinner. I'd deliver the fish to Maisie, who lifted her, as she prepared the roast, and know they would be served and stay uneaten, at tea.

My memory of her is more uncertain, probably because she died before it could harden. The large bed which must have been theirs before she fell ill, the rolls of toilet paper on the table to her left which her hand would make a handkerchief of when she coughed and the mounds of discarded paper on the floor, which Maisie would clear up, periodically. I assume now we were only let see her on her best days, which must have been infrequent. The bottles of perfume and quinine on the table, the smell of that perfume, which reminded me of churches, and a harsher odour, something medicinal. There were pictures ranged about the walls, of her with him, her with her numerous brothers, all with belts low and pot-bellies hanging over, hats at rakish angles, cigarettes hanging from lips and fingers.

She would smile weakly when I came in and I would resist the urge to snuggle up beside her, stand by the bedstead playing with the pearls she had draped round the metal, until her hand stretched over the pillow to grasp mine. Be a brave boy, Dony, she'd say and draw me slowly down to the bed, where some infant urge would take me over and I'd reach across the mounds of the quilt to clutch her shoulder and lie there, listening to both of us breathing. I would look from her face to the picture of her in her wedding dress, smiling, holding a bouquet, veil slightly askew, then to the one of him in his IRA uniform. I would ask her to tell me again the story of when the Tans came to catch him in the house near Mornington and she hid him among the potato drills and beat them out of the house with a broomstick.

He was from the country, she was from the city, and the difference for some reason seemed to me significant, though I didn't understand why. Her brothers would fill the house at weekends, ruffle my hair and press pennies in my hand and they spoke with a wit and a freedom that seemed to have passed him by. He would spend hours with her in the room, the door closed to any intrusion, nothing to indicate life inside but the low murmuring of their voices together. I would sit outside there, pulling wool from the carpet and rolling it into balls, like some guardian of their privacy. Or I would take the opportunity to wander through his office where the makeshift bed was that he slept in, the mass of papers on the green felt table by the window, the inkpot and the fountain pen, the sheafs of government notepaper and in the drawer beneath it, when I found the courage to open it, the gun in its leather shoulder-belt. It was significant in their union, I understood dimly, redolent of a time and a series of events that united them, despite her illness, despite his accent and the fact that he slept in the camp-bed by the corner. I would run my finger over its greasy surface and want to be beside her again, hearing her tell me of the Black and Tans, the potato drills and the broomstick.

I was clearing nightlines with him when the end came. Both of us barefoot again as we jerked the fishes' gullets from the hooks, whacked their heads on the hard sand, the white gills gasping and the cold blood streaming down my fingers when I looked up and saw Maisie on the promenade rubbing her hands in her smock with a distracted air and the doctor with the small black bag, running. Wait here, my father said, and he began to run too and I heard a strange cry from him as he ran, like an intake of breath or the squawk of a herring-gull as he left me with the handfuls of half-dead fish. I knew the immensity of it because he had left his shoes beside mine; it was most unlike that monument I thought my father was, scrambling over the layer of pebbles between the sand and the promenade wall. The tide was way out, so far out it seemed impossible that the thin white line by the horizon could have represented water. And it would be a dream I would have, many times later, the two of us walking towards the lines we had placed the night before. The nightlines in the dream would be so far out it seemed impossible we could have placed them but there, after all, they were, miles beyond the promenade wall, where the sand was sculpted in huge soft curves and the fish our hooks had gleaned were not the comforting plaice and sole we were used to, but odd misshapen creatures, pallid, translucent because of the depths they inhabited, huge whiskers and eyes, mouths shaped like tulips. We would approach these fish with circumspection, so unexpected were they, but they were fish after all, could be torn from the hooks and bleed like any others. And halfway through the work I would hear the roar, I would turn and see the white line of the sea had become a wall, bearing down on us and we would run from this tidal wave dragging fish, irons and catgut towards the distant haven of the promenade where the maid rubbed her hands on her smock with a distracted air and the doctor ran with unseemly haste towards the house.

But then I stood there with the fish; I knew I should follow but couldn't. I turned and walked towards the sea away from the house where what I didn't want to know was happening. They found me four hours later, by the rocky inlet round the Head. The tide had come in and my feet were bleeding from the stones. The black car pulled up by the road on the headland and Maisie walked from it. She clambered down the rocks towards me and said, You come home now. She's dead, isn't she, I said, and Maisie repeated, You come home now. So I went home.

So the light is up and the Moroccan is still banging his wooden support. It won't be long now till the priest walks out, stiff as he was last Sunday, alb and cincture blowing in the same wind. Here it's easy to imagine that nothing changes. The pattern of blood on what was once a monastery wall grows; each day another is shot and somehow nothing changes.

Death, I was to find, brought its privileges. As Maisie patched my knees and cleaned my feet she gave me gold-grain biscuits to quieten me. I sat by the warmth of the range and heard my voice coming out, piping, almost cheerful. She's dead, isn't she? Hush you, said Maisie, and

gave me a biscuit. Tears came to my eyes and she gave me
one more. And later, when I was brought upstairs, the
hush that fell on that sherry-filled room told me of a new
dignity I had been blessed with. The priest and all the un-
cles rose at once. I walked past the skirts of aunts with the
gravitas of an actor who knew his hour was come. I wept
when the priest touched my hair, wept more when the
priest stroked my cheek, and the tears were real, even
though they arrived on cue. The arms of the grandfather
clock held some strange fascination so I stared at them
rather than at the faces around me. They leapt forwards and
the chimes sounded. Father entered and stood with his face
by the window. I felt that we were vying for this moment
and that somehow I was winning hands down. Hand after
hand touched my cheek, pennies were pressed into my
palm and all I had to do was stand and weep. And my father
stood, stared out the window. His retiring soul kept the
grief intact and his reserve seemed shameful. He would
suffer with it for years, both the shame and the grief,
whereas I being young had only the grief and an adequate
stage upon which to display it.

Mouse came down later that evening. Mouse, who lived
in the cottage up in Bloodybank, who was brought up by
the aunt with the dyed blonde hair and the bedroom slip-
pers for shoes. He had been sent to get a bottle of milk by
his brother and had taken the longest of detours to get me
to come out. I could see from his expectant face under the
black hair that he hadn't heard the news. Come on, he said,
down the promenade to the amusements and to the corner
shop and back. I can't, I said, my eyes still wet. You leave
him be now, Maisie said, coming from the dark of the
10   kitchen with a tray of fruitcake. *Pourquoi,* said Mouse, who

liked big words. Maisie pulled me back and slammed the door and I tried to imagine the sang-froid with which he would accept the rebuff. Turning, shrugging, or walking backwards from the door, jingling the coins in his pocket. She drew me upstairs, the tray in one hand, my collar in the other, and introduced me to a roomful of a different set of mourners.

They drifted through for what seemed like days. The bell would ring and Maisie would run down and those I had known in other guises would enter, their faces now set in masks of condolence. Maisie kept an endless supply of fruitcake sashaying up the stairs, of cups of tea, glasses of sherry, goldgrain biscuits. After a while I must have fallen asleep for I remember being carried upstairs, the wool of his suit brushing off my cheek, an intimacy to which I was quite unaccustomed. He laid me down in the darkened room and said, Don't you worry about anything. I could see him standing above me and his cheeks were wet now, as if here he could allow himself tears. My voice came out calm and this surprised me, but now that we were alone, it was as if my show of grief could be let vanish. I won't, I said. We'll make do, he said, won't we? And there was that hint of uncertainty in his voice, as if maybe we wouldn't. We will, I said, and felt resentful at being the one who must provide the reassurance. What's my name? he asked me. It struck me as an odd question so I didn't answer for a bit and when he repeated it I said, You're my father. No, he said, what's my real name? Sam, I said. Your name's Sam. That's right, he said, and he wiped his cheek and left.

I lay awake for a while thinking about how everything had changed. He would later ask me about that time and about my memories of her, which grew dimmer as the years went on. I remember her well enough, I would say, to disguise that image I had of the bed in which she sat daily, surrounded by the paper into which she coughed. My one regret, he would say, is that she died before you got a chance to know her. The fact that this phrase, my one regret, became the prefix to many different statements, all of which he seemed to regret, did not pass me by. But I came to see that all of his regrets were centred round the one, the one he wept about as he stood in the bedroom and asked who he was, the one he felt as he deserted those fish and ran towards Maisie when that strange cry came out of him like a seagull's. I didn't know adults, I didn't know they could not state the obvious and only cry when alone. What I did know was that everything had changed and that my soul would change into a cold hard crystal because it had changed. I felt a sadness oozing out of me that I must dispel since I knew I must be free of it or live underneath its moisture for ever. It hovered above me like a departing soul and went out the window and I knew then that if she had gone anywhere it was into that sea from which we had plucked so many fish.

And I could see her as time went on gathering crusts of things the way objects do that are exposed to the tide. Things that have nothing to do with them: weed, shellfish and the dull green colour of copper when it rusts. Then again I would think the opposite: that she would become hard and smooth like a pebble or a piece of glass that loses its edges with the movement of the water, acquire the water's pale green colour, become something between water and stone. And I heard pebbles thrown against the window, as if to interrupt my thinking. I shook myself, walked out of bed in my communion suit and saw Mouse down below, throwing stones at the window.

C'est la vie, he said. He still had the empty bottle of milk in his hand. What does that mean? I asked him. Something deep, he said. Come on down, Dony, I'm in trouble. Why? I asked. Spent the money for the milk, he said, and I'm afraid to go home without it. As I climbed down he heard the money jingling in my pockets. By the sound of it, he said, you've got some spondulicks. I have, I told him, and when I reached the ground I emptied my pockets. I knew by now that he knew, but he would wait for me to mention it. Of uncertain parentage, he knew the etiquette of these things. So the money clinked, the coinage of the thing itself. There were four half-crowns and assorted six-pences. Where'd you get them? he wondered. People give you them when your ma dies, I said. He looked at me in the light coming from the upstairs window. His brown eyes like a cocker spaniel's, pale creamy face that made the lips too red and a lick of dark hair over the forehead. Mine were brown too, the hair was dark, but the skin was olive, like a foreigner's.

We walked across the sparse grass that led to the broken wall that led to the promenade. I'm sorry for your trouble, he said. But we must be thankful for small mercies. I didn't know mine. I didn't reply to this. I knew he spoke the way older kids spoke, for the sound of it mostly, and he mostly got the words wrong. We climbed over the broken wall and began running towards the lights of the amusements in the distance. But I stopped. I'd noticed something just beyond the line of the tide. Two poles sticking out of the water and a couple of shapes flapping between them.

He left his fish, I said and began to want to cry again.

What fish? Mouse asked.

Those ones. I pointed.

Ah come on, Dony, and he dragged at me again.

No. They're important.

And I clambered down towards them, into the water in my good suit, the shoes making a sucking noise each time I stepped. He stood at the edge, still jingling the coins.

What do you want them for? he asked.

For posterity, I said. It was a word I thought would have shut him up, since we both would have to pretend to understand it.

Ah yes, he said. The noise of the coins stopped. I grabbed both rods and dragged them out of the water. There were three plaice we hadn't yet unhooked. Their surprised eyes bulged and they shivered with their last pieces of life.

Got to go now, I said, dragging them behind me, towards the house.

I'm going to get it, Mouse said.

How much was the milk? I asked. I surprised myself, assuming control.

Sixpence, he said.

Here, I said, and held out my hand. He looked at me silently, his lips red in the moonlight, then he held out his. I took the coins and left him sixpence.

Don't go, Dony, he said. It was changing the rules somehow.

Have to, I said, and gave him another sixpence.

I walked back to the house and left him standing there by the water. Everything had changed, all right. When I got to the door, he was still there, looking up at me.

My father answered, dressed in his funeral suit.

You forgot these, I told him and held out the two rods and the dying fish. Sam.

They laid her out the next morning, in the upstairs living-room, in a dress that seemed to intimate a genteel party of some kind. My father held my hand and we both leaned forwards to kiss her perfect cheek. She looked younger in death, not sick any longer, but somehow distant, as if she was already sleeping beneath the tide that crept over our nightlines. Her brothers lifted the coffin and my father took his place up front. As he was taller than all four of them they had to stretch to keep some semblance of bal-ance. They walked gingerly down the stairs and out to the waiting car. We sat in the seat beside him and I watched through the window as the cortège drew off and every neighbour we passed removed his hat. Outside the church there was a crowd and each hat again came off. I saw Mouse, his school cap in his hand and his aunt's shock of yellow hair under a black bonnet. Again I felt numbed and oddly privileged. The wind blew from the Head, my un-cles strained to accommodate my father's height and only when we were seated inside, next to my tall, dark-suited father, and the priest walked through, coughing in his col-oured robes, did it strike me how fully gone she was.

Now that the sun has whatever meridian it needs to re-create that vulgar glory behind her head, the priest can make his entrance. The Garda Civil straighten their three-cornered hats and the soldiers begin their laconic march forwards. The coloured figure walks behind them, purple since it will be Easter soon, and behind him two peasant

15

soldiers dressed in white, one carrying the cruets, the other the makeshift altar. The Virgin flaps once more in the breeze, Mussolini flaps in turn and the tight-lipped Spaniard stays silent, as if he is today the stoic arbiter of the proceedings. The mackerel-ribbed magenta halo behind her holds its glory for one last beat and the wind is rising, whipping clouds of dust round the drab procession. The guards behind us fall to their knees and we stay standing. And maybe that was part of what brought me, tales of disinterred nuns waltzing in the arms of anarchists in Barcelona. I can see myself as Judas, he who betrays because he dimly perceives that was all that was expected of him. His stance in the living-room, preparing me for Mass, each Mass in memory of her, I suppose, his rigid expectation that I too would follow her precepts and the equally rigid certainty that I wouldn't. She had vanished, effected a trick more complete than any town-hall magician, he had moved his bed from his office back into the big brass bed where I used to lie with her and the string of pearls she had hung from the metal bars, her wedding and engagement rings now sat in the drawer, beside the gun and the shoulder-holster, mementoes of a marriage and a conflict of which he rarely spoke. Perhaps I missed her most for that, for the hints and stories she would give me of that past of theirs, bullets whacking past the chimney while the Irregulars and Free-Staters fought it out on the hills above.

And I realise that betrayal seeds itself, like a weed through a garden. His memory of his War of Independence was like the inviolate rose, ravished by the Civil War that followed. And fifteen years later, I joined a remnant of the splinters of that conflict, a wayward bunch of Republicans who, having exhausted the litany of betrayal at home, sought new possibilities abroad.

Come, Father, I should have whispered, talk to me, tell me why you so disapprove, show me the drama of your past, not your stiff present. You will kill him, Rose told me. Rose, who came to teach us piano and stayed. Maybe, I said, but I knew she was eluding me too. Whatever unspoken promise had been mooted on the piano keys had by now been forgotten, as if it had never existed. He has proposed to me, she said, her head leaning on the door jamb, the piano gleaming like a black seal behind her. He told me he would, I said to her. Her eyes wanted to know but I didn't continue. Hands gripping the green baize cardtable, the veins already bulging blue with the signs of age, eyes all avoidance. I am marrying, he told me, because it will be the best thing for all of us. How, Father? I asked him. Don't gall me, he said, you know how. But no, I told him, I honestly didn't. She has brought some peace to this place, he said, she's from a good family. What else? I asked him. The truth is, he said, and he looked suddenly tired, I've let you run wild. No, I told him, I've done that entirely on my own. Talk some sense to me, please, he asked. I've done the best I could, under the circumstances. And I thought if the circumstances were different, she might, we might, get along a bit better. So it'll be on her shoulders, I said. No, he said, it'll be on all our shoulders. This place hasn't been a home for fourteen years. And have you informed the lady? I asked him, and his hands shook, as if at an insult. Miss de Vrai, he said, is aware of my intentions. Thank God for that, I told him. I need your support, he said. Just tell me I'm right.

17

I stood there and said nothing. There was an obscenity at the heart of it I couldn't quite fathom. She is half your age, I wanted to say. Don't ask me to make your mind up for you, and I remembered what he said when he put me to bed the night she died. We'll make do, he said, won't we? There was the same question there, the need for reassurance. We didn't make do, I thought. But I repeated it anyway, wondering would he remember. We'll make do.

That night I played the piano while he tinkered with the fishing gear. She was due at seven. She would come in, I knew, with the knowledge that he had told me. Outside the sun was falling over the Irish Sea. The tide would soon be fully out and he would roll his trousers up to his calves and paddle out, with a spade and two rods and a tangle of lines. Some ritual was taking place, he wanted to be alone where I could see him, remembering that place we inhabited together years ago now, while I sat with her and somehow managed the knowledge of what he had told me. I tried to get the Ravel perfect while I heard the door below me close and heard the gate creak and soon saw him on the beach below, walking towards the line of retreated sea, looking for the casts the rags had left. He soon became a thin silhouette against the rage of colour in the evening sky behind. Then I heard the gate creak again and knew it was her. I heard the footsteps towards the door and saw the silhouetted figure digging furiously in the sand outside. Then the sound of the door opening and the footsteps up the stairs. I played, hitting wrong notes with my left, and wondered would my rendition of "Pavane for a Dead Infanta" somehow tell her that I knew.

Introibe ad altare, the priest begins, and I think it odd that they have the universal language while we aspire to the universal politics. The Welshman to my left chews a match and the two German youths stand bolt upright, as rigid in their opposition to the ceremony that is forced upon them as they would be in the observance. The wind has blown a fine layer of sand on to their faces, barely distinguishable from the pale down of their cheeks. They throw a glance sideways towards me, and I'm reminded again that they regard me with something like suspicion. Over the first weeks we lay on the hay on the stone floor under the vaulted ceiling of what must have been a wine-cellar and they talked about politics with a numb duty, as if only to remember what brought them here. In the beginning I answered dutifully but then, unable to stand their heroics any longer or even just possibly out of respect for a more mundane level of truth, I told them I came here because of all courses of action I could have taken it was the only one I knew with certainty that my father would have disapproved of. The words hung in the air, a dumb reality they knew, maybe, but would never admit.

So, though I stand with them now, I am suspect. I know in my heart the intimate rituals the priest circumscribes in the sandy air with his thin white hands. I welcome them secretly as a hint of home. I stand out of some obscure sense of fellowship but it is neither exhaustion nor the angular pebbles on the soles of my feet that make me want to kneel. I would slip downwards with relief, would welcome their contempt, would put myself outside once more another sphere of approval. And if I let my heart quicken the way it wants to, tears maybe would stream down my own sandy cheeks. I can remember those walks on Sunday down the promenade, both of us in our best suits, to the church on Sydney Parade. Those neighbours who passed us would nod, their faces set in what came to seem a permanent mask of condolence. The sea would change, from white-capped to still, steely grey, I would grow, my suit would change, my height would gain on his but the walk was sacrosanct and the hush of the church interior was always the same. I will go to the altar of God, to God the joy of my youth. There was a shocking relief in the silence there, in the knowledge that we could abide together amidst this ritual, and as with the nightlines, not have to blunder towards speech. So I came to think of God as a great mass of quiet, a silence that was happy with itself, a closed mouth. Till the time came when I would interrupt that quiet.

I remember Mouse, his face perplexed and saddened among the surging crowds who tried to block us from the boat on Eden Quay.

He walked with me from the house towards Bray station, past the sea to our left and the large Victorian piles to our right. He reminded me of the hawker we'd seen in Greystones, scattering broken glass out of a sack to gather the crowds. We'd bet our souls on whether he would bleed when he lay on them. You won, Mouse, I told him. Nobody wins a bet like that, he said. We turned up from the sea by the Northern Hotel past the Legio Maria pebbledash front with the Virgin holding the ball of the known world, towards the train. What'll he do without you? Mouse said. He had come to be more Christian than I. He'll have her, I told him. And more to the point, what will you do without me? He sniffed in the cold air and brushed his black hair from his perfect forehead. I'm going for prelims next month, he said. He would pretend to me his application to a seminary was to provide him with a cheap degree, but I knew the reality. He had found God with a vengeance. And then? I asked him, lying, as he wanted me to. Maybe teaching. The train came and I said, You don't have to come any farther. Why not? he asked. There'll be a demonstration at the boat, I told him. You shouldn't be seen with the likes of me. But he shut me up with a glance of contempt and opened the carriage door.

Rose had declined to come that day and my father had stood by the living-room window, with his face turned to the sea once more. You're too young, he said, to take a step like this. Was I ever too young? I asked him. Why do you think you're so different? he asked me. I don't, I said. You don't choose conflict, he said, war and hate and all that, it chooses you. So it chose you once, I said. That was different, he said. What I can't take any more, I said, is the hypocrisy, the prevarication—Don't give me politics, he said, I know all that. Just tell me what it is. You know what it is, I told him. I don't, he said, I honestly don't. Then look at me and tell me that, I asked him. But I turned and left before he had a chance to.

You've got him wrong, Mouse said as the train soughed past Killiney. Maybe, I said, but doing something is better than nothing. What do you mean? Mouse asked. The heroic act, I told him, is as apt a metaphor as any for this condition we call life. The contemplation of it sweet, the execution tortuous and the end product vacuous. You'll have to translate for me, said Mouse. If I stayed what would I do? I asked him. Stay in that house where every-   **21** thing is intimated, nothing ever said. Wait for that wedding which neither of them will mention. Wish them off to some drab hole like Brighton and wait for them to return again. You know I can't live here . . .

What if you're wrong? he asked.

But I couldn't accept that possibility so came out with the grander reasons, the rotten core of the bourgeoisie, the need to obviate one's class in the broader struggle, how any action at all is better than paralysis, but I could tell he wasn't listening, I could tell that stuff meant nothing to him. I watched his profile against the glass with all the eucalyptus of Killiney hill going past and knew he wasn't made for those kinds of abstraction. His eyes were silver with the light behind him and his cheek seemed wet.

It's her, isn't it, he said.

What's her? I asked.

You can't stand the thought of him and her.

I turned away but it didn't matter, he knew he had struck home.

They called out the banns in the windswept church on the hill where he had married once before. I hadn't been there but Mouse told me of them and I told him he should have come up with some reasons for objection. What ones? he asked. On the grounds, I told him, of the ridiculous. She kept the brochures for her wedding trousseau half hidden in her music case. I thought of searching in his desk for the ring, hidden I imagined among the yellowing journals where he kept the newspaper cuttings of his contributions to the Treaty debates, but decided against it. The silence in the house said everything. A silence different from before, a congealed pall of the unspoken. I would pass him on the stairs, her on the promenade, and one day decided it was simpler to leave.

I want my absence, I told Mouse, to be a more effective damnation than my presence could ever have been. With me there, they can cough and shuffle, imagine my presence is a barrier to speech. With me gone, they will be left with the reality of it.

And what's that? Mouse asked.

Ridiculous, I said.

When we came to Westland Row and made it to the quays the crowds were all around us. I looked at the sad bunch coming out of Liberty Hall under the ITGWU banner. He had belonged to the same union once, walked out of the same hall, his Trinity scarf like a beacon among the mufflers, before he chose more staid political realities. I made my way towards them and was about to say goodbye but the crowds surged forwards, spitting blood and rosaries. Mouse was swept beyond me, part of them now without wanting to be. He pushed forwards and got the bag into my hands and tried to say something but the crowds pulled him beyond me. And I walked under the drab banner and felt the spittle or maybe it was the spray on my face, for the wind was up and the boat was pitching, and as we walked up the swaying gangplank I turned and saw him in his black gabardine coat, pressed between a mass of women on their knees, rosaries raised in their fingers, and he tried to wave his hand but couldn't so he smiled, as if only now conscious of the joke at the heart of it all.

Lord I love the beauty of Thy house, the priest says, and the place where Thy glory dwells. As the boat drew towards the Kish lighthouse I could see the house one last time, the roofs perched above the thin fawn pencil of Bray harbour, barely visible in the mist. A line of three-storeyed late Georgian dwellings at right angles to the sea. With a balcony running the length of them, adding a touch of rococo, white-painted, peeling, sagging under the weight of hard winters. Ours second from the end, protected somewhat from the waves that buffeted them, worst when the tide was high and the wind from the east. A small ledge running the length of them too to prevent flooding. The view was of a promenade, a long stretch of green and concrete leading to Bray Head with a railing to frame the ocean running its length, painted blue sometimes, mucous green at others. A bandstand, quite proud of itself, smack in the middle. The shape of this bandstand, with its top like a Chinaman's hat, was echoed intermittently down the length of the prom by gazebos, follies, small shelters, call them what you will, perched somewhere between utilitarian and purely decorative functions.

Why he chose that house I will never know, it was too small for one of his Protestant Ascendancy background, too large for one of hers. He would have been by then a veteran of the War of Independence, a fact I would have been inordinately proud of, if he allowed me, if he allowed himself a hint of the same. My mother was from Dorset Street and the pictures he kept of her show a rolling Edwardian glamour not too far removed from the music-hall. They must have been miles apart, aeons, centuries, light-years, if I can judge from the pictures, my own uncertain memories and the uncles that I met, in cinemas, at race meetings, the dogs, places he would rarely have gone. All of them small, with a swagger dictated by the rolling belly, conversation scattered from the left-hand corner of the mouth, between drags of a cigarette, a short rasping cough and a quick guffaw. They met during the Black and Tan War. She was nineteen, spending her summer in her uncle's farm in Mornington on the mouth of the Boyne. The uncle kept a safe house; he was billeted on it in the way of those days, came in the dead of night, wet, his Mauser tucked in his greatcoat, and slept in a chicken-coop. She blundered in to collect the eggs next morning and found him in the arms of Morpheus among the flying feathers. She cooked him breakfast and that, I suppose, was that. I like to think of her in a cardigan, the rough hem of her dress dangling over a pair of Wellington boots, a young impressionable girl with a tomboy's face, a pair of eggs in her hand, entranced with this figure half covered in hay and chickenshit. He took to visiting her, during the long winter that built up to the Truce, in that redbricked slum in Dorset Street. The erratic nature of his visits, the roman-tic allure of the gunman fastening round her heart, I sup-pose.

The differences in their nature were left dormant, to emerge. A Trinity student, he became a convert, in more ways than one. To the Republican creed of those days, and then, before his marriage, to Catholicism. They married during the Truce and honeymooned during the Treaty de-bates, and a certain greyness must have entered his soul as he watched the rhetoric of betrayal lead inexorably to-wards civil war. Perhaps it was exhaustion that led him to take the Free State side, and perhaps again it was the pull of his background.

He bought the house before the marriage, I learnt later from the title deeds. She was to die within five years of coming, so it was destined to be her only one. And again I can imagine her first view of it, from the train that would have brought her from Dublin, the harbour and the boat-works behind it swinging past, then the row of houses and the balconies revealing themselves from a sideways perspective that gradually became flat, like a painted postcard. Dishevelled, mid-Victorian, comfortable somehow like the skirts of aunts or a game of bowls on a Sunday afternoon. The peeling white paint of the wooden balconies, the sea beating behind, the brown length of the harbour wall and the shell of the Turkish baths on the ocean side. Did she know she was to die in it, I often wondered, that the regular thump of the waves on the promenade would accompany her last heartbeat? When she opened the front door for the first time and sunlight disturbed the dust the last owners had left, and saw the fleur-de-lis on the linoleum floor, did she make a mental note to replace it? If so she never got round to it, for its prosaic ugliness dominated my childhood. The pair of small white high heels with the pearls where the laces should be would have left neat prints on the dust over the linoleum, since I can't imagine him lifting her in the way that tradition demanded. But then again maybe he did, maybe there was a strong, reassuring forearm under the small of her back, the folds and laces of a wedding dress tucked underneath his palm, her lips and chin embedded in his neck, beardless, since the beard came later.

A foghorn blaring through their first night in that house together. Announcing the mists that would surround it, creep up to the ground-floor windows from the sea beyond. The mists I can imagine would envelop it like a glove, seep through the cracks in the window-panes and drop the temperature inside so she could clutch him more ardently in the brass bed she was to die in.

Confiteor tibi in cithara, Deus, Deus meus. The words are carried on the wind which raises another cloud of dust and the Virgin shudders with her melancholy smile. I will praise thee upon the harp, O God, my God. Why art thou sad, O my soul? and why dost thou disquiet me? There was a piano in the front living-room which I have a dim memory of her playing. Some wet afternoons I would hear the keys tinkle again and imagine she had come back, picture the keys moving of their own accord. I would creep downstairs, the random arpeggios creating chords I'd never heard before, then see Maisie through the half-open door, brushing the notes with her dustcloth. Maisie made a poor substitute for even the hope of her presence, but sometimes at night when the wind whistled through the sails in the harbour outside my bedroom window I would mistake the sounds for music. I would creep down again, in darkness this time, and see the keys gleaming in the moonlight, untouched. I would tinker with them, become her ghost myself, pick out the melodies I most wanted to hear. "Roll Out the Barrel," "Roses Are Blooming in Picardy," "The Harp That Once Through Tara's Halls." The piano became my way to her, till one night a shadow crossed the moonlight over the keys and I felt the hair stipple on my back. I stayed still, my hands holding the dying notes until the shadow moved to my left and I heard the cough behind me and realised it was him. Where did you learn to play? he asked. I didn't, I said, afraid to turn. You make a good hand at it, he said, and came towards me and his voice was

27

hoarse. I thought it was her, he said. I lifted my hands from the keys and listened to the silence, realising it had been years since he mentioned her, and still not by name.

I have hired you a teacher, he said soon after. Miss de Vrai, and I imagined a thin spinster in a tartan dress, clutching a ruler with which she could rap my knuckles. But what came was Rose. Rose, whom I first saw from the top window, her damp hair lifted in the wind like a flock of starlings. It was just after a spring tide and it was spring too, for the waves were crashing with celebrative bursts along the whole length of the promenade. She clutched her gabardine coat around her, held her music case up to protect her face from the spray and laughed as she struggled with the wind. I understood that laugh, I'd seen it on kids, indulged in it myself, being a kid, but had rarely seen it on adults. A wave hit her, nearly knocked her sideways, and she stopped a moment to regain her breath. I knew she was bound for our house, by the music case. So she gripped one hand against the railings, her hair wet, the gabardine clinging to her body. She moved to dodge the next wave and walked straight into another and laughed again. She looked up at the house, and I wondered could she see me in the upstairs window. She moved to safer terrain then, and walked on. I tried to imagine what the house would look like to her, a line of peeling façades, buffeted by wind and water, at the farther end of the promenade. I saw her cross the grass verge then, by the broken wall that was meant to protect the green from floods; she tried to pick her way through the numerous pools, then gave up, and simply walked, the water coming up to her ankles over her laced boots. I wondered whether I should shout to Maisie that she was here. Then I heard the doorbell ring and heard

Maisie running anyway to answer it. I walked out of my room to the top of the stairs and looked down. Maisie was ushering her in and the wind slammed the door behind her, leaving her in a small damp patch of her own making. Maisie ran to get towels, gave one to her and dabbed the carpet with the other.

So where are they? she asked, her face invisible under the towel.

Dry yourself first, said Maisie. Plenty of time. She drew her inside the kitchen as I came down the stairs. When I reached the ground floor the door was shut. I could hear voices from inside it, Maisie with her high Wicklow whine and hers, which seemed to have the softness of the west coast about it. I opened the door slowly with my foot, wanting to see but not wanting to be seen yet, and saw Maisie wrapping one of my father's coats around her, her skirt and stockings hanging round the stove.

So I should have known, I suppose, even then: the drizzle-filled accent, her head bent so her straw-coloured hair could catch the heat, wearing my father's coat. I should have foreseen, with the instinct which, if it were given to any of us, would save all manner of trouble, would let us know which door to open and which to leave closed, which corridor to walk down and blunder towards the light. But I doubt if it would have made any difference, maybe only made the possibilities more alluring, more forbidden, and besides, how could I have connected him with this easily natural creature, running her fingers through her dampened hair, turning to greet me with a wry, cracked smile and saying, And you must be Donal.

I blushed at the mention of my name. Every child hates their name, I discovered later, hates the present they have been given, imagines others far more potent and alluring. Then I saw the stockings and thought my embarrassment might be misinterpreted, so blushed again.

He's a shy one, she said, walking towards me, wrapping my father's coat around her waist.

Still waters run deep, said Maisie.

They do, she said, and held out her hand. I'm Rose.

I shook her hand and smiled and said, Hello, Rose, and with the sound of my own voice gathered mastery of myself once more. You've come to teach us piano.

That I have, Donal, she said. When do I start?

I would have said now, but Maisie shooed me out, told me Miss de Vrai needed time to make herself respectable, whereupon Rose laughed as if such words hardly applied to her and Maisie shut the kitchen door.

I walked back up the stairs and sat in the living-room. I could see the waves crashing down the length of the promenade. I decided only someone exceptional would let themselves get that wet. Only someone exceptional would wrap a man's coat around them, dry their hair in front of me by the stove and smile even though her stockings were drying on it. I heard footsteps below then and the tinkle of a cascade of scales, light and rapid, the waves outside thrusting up in some odd counterpoint. I became aware, slowly, that some new principle had entered the household, some new element that made me apprehensive and excitable all at once. After a time the music stopped and Maisie's feet trudged up the stairs and I understood I had been summoned.

You behave yourself, Maisie said, ushering me downwards.

30   Why wouldn't I? I asked her.

When I came down my father's coat was draped round the wicker chair and she was sitting by the piano in a flower-patterned dress, rippling up and down it like a concert pianist, her head thrown back and her damp hair hanging down her shoulders. She looked up when I entered, but kept playing. She smiled, said my name silently and gestured with her head for me to sit beside her. I sat down as close as was comfortable and imagined I got the smell of roses from her, but that could have been her name.

Rose, I said.

That's my name, she said, still playing.

Where are you from, Rose? I asked her.

A place near Sligo, she said. Strandhill.

What's it like?

Like here, she said. Only the waves are bigger.

So I understood the way she stood on the promenade when the water ran its fingers down her. She was used to hurricanes.

Where did you learn to play like that, Rose?

School of Music, she said. In Chatham Street.

That in Dublin?

Yes. She still played.

You live in Dublin, Rose?

Unfortunately.

Where's your family then?

Aren't you the curious one, Donal.

Must be.

Then her fingers stopped.

So show me, she said.

I played "The Harp That Once Through Tara's Halls." I was inordinately proud of my mastery of it, so was stunned when I finished and she said nothing.

Well? I asked her. I looked up and saw her staring out the window.

Good, Donal, she said. Good. She opened her bag and took a small metronome out and set it clicking on the piano. Try it again, and watch the timing.

There was light rain falling when she left, the kind that created a veil over the head, and the waves had died down. I assumed the tide had changed. She put her music case over her head again and walked through it, in her newly dry gabardine coat. I saw a figure come down the promenade towards her, carrying a briefcase, and knew it was my father, coming home from work. I saw her walk towards him, oblivious, about to pass him when she stopped, summoned by him, I suppose. They talked for a moment, then she went on. I assumed he must have known her, searched out an ad in the *Irish Times,* walked to the Music School in Chatham Street, questioned her credentials, from the way they spoke. I allowed myself to be jealous for a moment, a warm feeling, creating both need and sadness, with the rain falling round them, her stopping, raising her head from under the music case, a moment of recognition, him stiff against the railings, the sea moving in big slow swells behind them. Then she smiled, placed the case over her head again and walked on. He watched her go, I watched the two of them, then he turned, allowed his cane to rattle off the railings as he walked.

Confiteor Deo omnipotenti, he says, and the wind and the hammering carry away his words, but I hardly have to hear them, I know them so well the litany carries on regardless. *Beatae Mariae, semper Virgini.* I could confess that I wanted her then, but that would be an untruth, or a truth after the

32

fact, a retrospective lie. I was too young to know such things, was glad of a feminine presence other than Maisie in the house, wished to reinvent the mother I had lost perhaps, wished to complete this household in a way I'd never known. So maybe that would be the retrospective truth, the posthumous truth that when I saw them greet each other on the promenade through the patina of rain I hoped that something in her would gladden him. In the way that children have, their knowledge that something is important, beyond their comprehension, but they cling to it and build upon it and work to fill the gaps they feel are missing.

She came regularly, on Tuesdays and on Thursdays, and the music was secondary to the feel of her hair brushing off my cheek, the half-attentive way she listened, the way when I'd finished a piece I'd turn, see her sitting by the window, quite forgetful of the fact that I was there at all. Then she'd come to and whisper, Good, Donal, good, better every day, talk of the left hand or the right and once, or if I was lucky twice, during a lesson would come behind me, grip one hand and show me how to hold my wrist. There were no rings on her fingers, which I knew was significant. Much more significant was the smell of her hair as it brushed off my cheeks, the feel of her breasts pushing into the small of my back. There was an eroticism there which was undefined, which I would always connect with the stark glory of a Bach prelude, which even now I could not call desire. It gave me balance and poise, completed me, or more properly, completed the house. That cold structure, perched on the edge of the Irish Sea, seemed warmer for it. I allowed myself to wonder would my mother have been like this, had she lived. I lost the memory of the bed surrounded by crumpled paper, the cold

33

imagined grave at the bottom of the sea. I remembered a younger woman now, unencumbered by sickness, hair with a hint of red, in a gabardine coat. They were the happiest days, looking back on it, me, him and her, twice a week. He took to coming home early on the days of her lessons. He would ask about our progress, hold her coat for her as she went to the door, sometimes walk her to the station.

The way it goes, said Mouse, as we followed their silhouetted figures on the promenade from the shore below, is that the gentleman takes the lady's hand.

How? I asked him.

Like this, he said, slipping his arm through mine. I could see my father's hand above though, wrapped chastely round her music case, a gap of blue air between his shape and hers. Perhaps the feel of the scuffed leather gave him the same pleasure as ran through me when Mouse's fingers curled into mine.

It's called stepping out, he said. Courting. The bit before the other bit begins.

And what's the other bit? I asked, though I already suspected.

The gentleman, he said, gathers the courage to kiss the lady.

Aha, I said. Try as I would, I could never imagine my father's lips on hers.

He blushes, said Mouse, coming to a halt. And the lady's heart flutters. Then he goes for it.

He placed his red lips on mine, not blushing at all. I could feel the breath from his nostrils on my cheek. Then his tongue came through them and played with mine.

What's the tongue for? I asked, squirming away.

That leads to the next bit, he said.

There's even more bits? I asked.

Bit after bit after bit, he said, one leading to the other till the gentleman gets his bit.

His bit, I said.

Yeah, but that comes much later.

I looked up and saw their figures vanishing under the bridge.

Come on, I said. Let's see what bit they get to.

I followed him up the broken stone steps with a heavy heart. We climbed the footbridge and saw their figures vanish behind the railway station, then emerge by the tracks, standing under the dripping eaves. The thought of his lips on hers made me feel sadder than I had ever felt. Then the train came in and enveloped them in steam. We saw him standing stiffly, bowing slightly as he handed her the case. The thought came again, of his lips on hers, but nothing in his body suggested it. I felt sorry for him suddenly, realising he'd never get to the first bit, even. Then the other sorrow came back to me at the thought that he might. The sorrow rattled between us, like the doors of the train as it shuddered into movement. Then it drew off slowly and he turned to watch it go and Mouse dragged me down beneath the rail to hide. The train trundled beneath us, enveloping us in a cloud of smoke.

No go, whispered Mouse.

He had gone when the smoke cleared and the wisps of it vanished from the tracks like the sadness.

Misereatur vestri omnipotens Deus, the priest intones and the wind whips the surplice of the kneeling altar-boys and I can see two pistols stuck behind two leather belts. That walk of theirs became a regular occurrence, whenever he was home early enough to meet her, and when the rains came he would carry an umbrella. His courtship, if that's what it was, would progress to holding her arm when the winds were high and the waves crashed over the railings. I watched every gesture, sometimes from my bedroom window, sometimes from the beach below. Mouse would design appropriate futures for them both. The day would come, he would tell me, when some cataclysm would prevent the train from arriving and they would wait at the station till the light went. He would walk her back, all hope of the journey to Dublin vanished, back along the promenade to the front door. And then? I asked him. Then, Mouse said, Maisie, acting on some instinct for such disasters, would have a tea ready. A tea for three. You, her and him, Mouse said. I tried to imagine the scene, with a catch in my throat. You would eat boiled eggs on the table by the kitchen range and she would stay the night. Where? I asked, with an unerring eye for such details. It doesn't matter where, he told me. On the contrary, I said, it matters a lot. On the couch by the piano, I said, preferring to keep her near my element. A lady can't sleep on a couch. On the contrary, I told him, echoing his diction, a lady can, on that couch. It pulls out into a settee. And then? he asked. Then, I said, we would have breakfast the next morning. More boiled eggs, he said. Fried ones, I told him. Fried ones with bacon. Then, he said, the sun would be up and they'd walk down to the station again. But nothing would be as it seems. Why not? I asked. During the night, he told me, everything would have changed. He walks

down the promenade with no need to protect her from the

wind but yet with his arm around her. Why would it have changed? I asked him. And he must have sensed my disturbance, for he didn't reply.

The train would never come, I told him. The tide would go out and never come back. They would wait hours by the station and come back that night and I'd pull out the couch for her and she'd sleep on the settee once more. She'll teach me the next morning and every morning after till I can play like Chopin. Who was he? asked Mouse. A Pole, I told him, with long fingers who had a way with the ladies. And where's your father? Out, I said. Always out, trying to find where the sea has gone.

You're lying, said Mouse. How'm I lying? I asked him. You'll be the one out there, trying to find where the sea is gone. No, I said, you're the one who's lying. How? he asked. You know, I said, that the train always comes.

Though their walk remained as chaste as ever, as the hot days came down on us Mouse and I invented an erotic history for them. We would swim in the afternoons, then lie naked on the rocks before the Head, see their tiny figures on the promenade below. We would twine bodies, as he told me they one day would, our pricks hard against each other's legs. We'd kiss and go through the inventory of gestures men went through with women. It was fine to imagine Mouse as her and him as me and I'd scour the roof of his mouth with my tongue to keep the sadness at bay. I could imagine an erotic thread interlacing the four of us like a necklace, stretching the length of the hot promenade. I wanted him outside of it, yet somehow part of it, an arbiter of the affections and pleasures I knew were properly mine.

The weekends between the lessons were filled with her

absence. He would take the fishing lines out from beneath the stairs while I practised the scales she had given me till I would hear the front gate open and the scraping of the metal rods off the concrete outside. I would see him through the window, untangling the hooks from the cat-gut, and know they would remain knotted till I made my way outside to join him. The tide is good, he would say, and hand me one rod which I would walk backwards with as the skein unravelled. Then we'd walk across the scutched grass to the broken parapet that led to the prome-nade with the hooks swinging between us. You were prac-tising, he'd say, leaving a hint of her in the warm air. Yes, I would answer, and want to talk about her but feel the weight of his reserve. So I'd look at the thin line of the sea instead and wonder would we come out the next morning to find her entangled in the lines, like a mermaid, mine for the whole weekend.

Then the day came when they walked the promenade and every lamppost was emblazoned with a poster advertis-ing his face. I had long come to understand the probable significance of the handgun he kept in the spare room, among my mother's things. He had been born a Protestant but converted to Catholicism at the time of his marriage. Betrayal, then, began with him. He had betrayed the inter-ests of his Ascendancy class by joining the Republican movement. When the War of Independence gave way to the Civil War, he felt betrayed by that Republican move-ment in turn. He joined the Treaty side, was given a post in the first Cosgrave administration, and there his slow drift back to the politics of his class began. One of the few of Protestant background in the Free State government, his

38

presence would have given some comfort to the disaffected of his own class. So he presided, in part, over the incarceration and decimation of his former comrades. I had heard him mutter darkly about De Valera as the embodiment of satanic guile, as the murderer of one Michael Collins. He had seen the same De Valera spend years in the outer wilderness of non-participation in the electoral process, and then march back with his followers into the Dáil, one hand on the book, reciting the oath of allegiance, the other on the guns inside their coat pockets. He went for election again in 1932, in West Wicklow, his military past and his Ascendancy present presumably a bulwark against the rising tide of Republicanism. So for the following summer, the Wicklow landscape became synonymous with my father's face. It was plastered on to stone walls, nailed on to trees, flapping outside churches; the rains sweeping down from the Sugarloaf gave his image the texture of whatever surface it covered. I saw him speak from the bandstand through a megaphone, in halting tones more suited to the proceedings of the Royal Dublin Society than to the group of windswept weekenders that congregated on the promenade in front of him. He campaigned with a decorum that must have been unique to his constituents, in all weathers, outside churches, pubs, football pitches, and one morning the gaunt, iconic figure of De Valera himself harangued the Mass-goers from one side of the church railings, my father from the other. I glimpsed it with Mouse as we filed inside and knew even then how unequal a contest it was. When we came out, all that remained of the encounter was a road filled with pamphlets and the posters of my father's face flapping against the church railings. Do you think he won? I asked Mouse, not quite versed in electoral procedures. I think they were just the heats, he said; the big game is later.

Though he lost, needless to say, along with his party. Rose came to teach us on the day the results came in and was unusually subdued. I played for a while and she hardly listened. Then she placed her hand over mine on the keyboard and asked me where he was. In his study, I told her, looking at the freckles of her muscular hand on mine. Go up and talk to him, she said. About what? I asked her. Whatever, she said, just go and talk to him.

So I left the piano and walked upstairs. I knocked on his door and when there was no answer, pushed it open slightly. The floor was strewn with newspapers; he was sitting at the green card-table by the window, smoking a cigarette. Is there anything up? I asked him. No, he said, nothing's up. What are you doing then? I asked him. I was listening, he said. He pushed his glasses off his forehead and looked at me. I had so rarely seen his eyes without the opaque glass in front of them that I was surprised by their startling blue. We might be in trouble, he said to me. Because you lost? I asked him. Yes, he said. Won't Dev give you a job? I asked him; and he smiled at my naivety. Dev, he said, wouldn't give me the time of day. Didn't you know him once? I asked. More than that, he said. He was my chief. So what happened then? I asked him. We fought, he said, but that's all over now. Tell me about it, I asked him, since like any kid I longed to know about the gun and the blood it had spilt. No, he said, you wouldn't understand. Go down and finish your lesson.

40   So I went down and played again. I was aware he was

listening and took care to finish every phrase, to anticipate mistakes, to keep the pedal down so the notes would carry upstairs. I had progressed to Schubert by then and tried to fill the house with it. When I had finished, there was silence, from upstairs and from Rose beside me. I turned to look at her, expecting some comment, but her head was tilted back, her eyes looking up to the ceiling and her hair hanging free like a curtain behind her. She said nothing for a while.

What do you think would make him happy? she asked me eventually.

You, I was about to say, but didn't.

A job, I said.

To his surprise, though, he was given a job. Whether it was a sudden softening in the harsh deity De Valera had become or the fact that the new administration needed some semblance of continuity, he was appointed to the post of under-secretary to the Department of External Affairs. Whatever the cause, he was absent from the house now consistently, returning long after nightfall.

So his defeat had one happy outcome. I got to walk Rose down the promenade to the train. The sky was an expanse of silver over the mottled sea. I was taking his place, I felt, *in loco parentis,* and tried to fulfil my role with all the gestures at my disposal. I carried her music case, a touch I was proud of since I'd never seen him do it. I held her elbow as we crossed the pools of brine on the grass, making our way up to the level-crossing. Won't be long now, I said, in my best adult manner as she leaned her head against the station wall, waiting for her train. His election poster curled round every pillar in the station as the train drew off, flapping in the wind the carriage left behind it, the way those three huge visages do now. It had the same distant authority, the same melancholy, the same sense of loss.

Over the next weeks the posters decayed, became sodden with rain, torn at the corners, wedding themselves eventually to the brick and metal surfaces they sat on. He grew into the landscape, became part of it, of the gazebos, the lampposts, the stone-pillared shelters, of the promenade I walked down towards the train with Rose.

That became my job and I its diligent servant. Touching her elbow, passing the bandstand, to which the weather had welded the remnants of his face. Rose? I would ask her. Yes, Donal, she would answer in a way that became an obligatory litany for our conversations. What kind of house did you grow up in in Sligo? A cottage, she would tell me, beside a golf course that backed on to the sea. And, Rose? I would say again. Yes, Donal, she would answer. Are your sisters anything like you? Two of them are, she would tell me, and two of them aren't. And the ones that aren't, Rose, I would ask. What do they look like? Sheila, she would tell me, looked good till she married the farmer but now she's bigger than a haycart. And Joan was born to be a spinster, so she's thin. Were you born to be a spinster, Rose? I would ask her, knowing she would bless herself and give her special smile. And, Rose? I would ask. Yes, Donal, she would answer. Tell me their names again. Sheila, Joan, Fergus, Johnnie, Angela, Mary and Pat. That's seven, Rose, I would say. Eight, she'd tell me, including me.

Because every detail of her background fascinated me, more than the lessons, maybe even more than her head of hair. The cottage I could picture, the golf course where they picked balls from the rough and sold them back to golfers at twelve a penny, the beach she described to me with the sand-dunes and the curling breakers, but I could never see the legions of sisters and brothers inside the cottage, only her. A cottage with a tin roof which the rains played on like a kettle-drum and her inside, sitting at a piano among the bric-à-brac. Though I later learnt there was no piano, she had learnt on the upright in the priest's house, then graduated to playing organ at Mass on Sundays, won a scholarship to Dublin and stayed at a hostel run by nuns in Leeson Street. But what matter, we should be able to choose the pasts of those around us: I would have had her in bare feet, an only child, walking that beach and golf course endlessly, a lover of twilights, aware of a grander destiny than was implied by her simple surroundings. We would reach the station then and she'd lean on the green pillar as the five-thirty came in from Greystones, she'd pat me on the cheek, tell me to practise and be gone in an expanse of railway carriages.

The sun has become proper daylight now and the winds have died a bit. The priest turns and raises his fingers and rivers of sweat are running down his forehead. It is possible almost to feel sympathy for him in that board-like purple outfit, in front of this stolid congregation. He is reaching up to his moment, I imagine, when the pale hands take the small white disc and the mundane miracle happens. The Welshman to my left looks at me sideways, imagining my response. He knows everything, I imagine for a moment, with his small miner's eyes, his rock-like common sense. So what's a Mick doing here? he asks me with monotonous regularity. Passing the time, I tell him. I fancy the heat to disguise the fact that I know he knows I'm not one of them. Something in my face shows it, I suppose, some comfort emanates to me from the altar beyond us on the packing cases, the wine the priest pours from the leather gourd into the cruets, and I wonder when he lifts the tiny disc between both thumbs and forefingers will I be able to resist the urge to kneel. My apostasy is almost over.

She became a friend. I suppose that's the word for it—the gap between our ages wasn't that great; she would have been nineteen, pushing twenty, when I reached fourteen. I was a quick pupil, had a strong mimetic ability, came to copy every movement of her hands and came to see in the end that her facility was limited. The pieces we played became like duets. She tried to disguise the fact that I was gaining on her and I tried to hold myself back. But one day working on the Schumann I must have forgotten myself and played the whole thing, from start to finish, her turning the pages, saying nothing for a full twenty minutes. Then the piece was over and I remembered. I looked at her, a deep blush spreading over her cheeks, and cursed myself silently.

You know what it is, she said.

What? I asked her.

You don't need me any longer, she said.

Why not? I asked her.

Because I can't get through that.

Can you keep it a secret? I asked her.

Now why would I do that? she asked.

Because I want you to stay, I was thinking, because he wants you to stay.

Because you need the money, I said, shooting in the dark.

She smiled, embarrassed, and I realised that I was right.

Because I need you to listen, I said. If you didn't teach me, I wouldn't play.

She said nothing and the smile slowly faded.

That was a fluke, I said, growing desperate. Then she stood up.

Please, I said, and I grabbed her hand to stop her. My arm was across her stomach. She placed her other hand over mine and held it, warmly, kneading the fingers. I felt a deep blush flooding my cheeks, but she didn't seem to notice.

I could hear Maisie moving around upstairs. Rose's fingers kept that ripple over mine and I realised we were talking about the lessons no longer. And slowly the blush on my face receded. She turned, took my head in her hands and kissed me on the cheek.

Don't worry, Donal, she said. I'm going nowhere. Anyways, I can't afford to. I stayed still, feeling her lips close, her breath on my cheek, and wondering what I would have done if she had been Mouse.

You can teach me, she said, hardly moving a muscle. I could hear Maisie's feet coming down the stairs, and she drew away.

Now play it again, she said.

Hoc est enim corpus meum, the priest says and now raises the small disc of white. The Virgin seems to sweat in the heat and Mussolini stares into some indeterminate future and the Caudillo contemplates his own moustache. And I feel the urge to kneel, if only for my father's sake, but the Welshman spits contemptuously to the pebbles in front of him and the Spaniard who tries to crawl into my bed each night cracks a thin, melancholy smile.

He left us to our own devices, as his face on the posts of the promenade urinal became gradually indistinguishable from the concrete. Rose stayed, I can only surmise because she had to, because of those seven brothers and sisters in that cottage in Sligo, because prospects for young ladies were limited. Some years later I would visit out of curiosity the hostel where she lived in Hatch Street and understand more: the barred windows, the nuns in blue, the list of rules pasted on the inside door. But at the time I imagined she'd stayed because of me. The thought of her complementing my father's life had vanished; he was rarely there. She began to complement mine. I came to understand the precise emotional import of those stockings, drying by the stove that day I first met her. I discovered Erik Satie. The arbitrary melodies puzzled her, but she worked her way through them while I stood behind her, watching the movement of her shoulders under her dress. I could see between her buttons the down of her skin. I reached my finger out to touch that skin, expecting a reprimand, or the music to stop. But none of that happened; she stiffened slightly, then relaxed and played on. This then became our habit: Erik Satie, her working out the discords as I sat beside her and worked my hand up the inside of her leg. Stop it, Donal, she would mutter, but some peasant pleasure-principle took over, her knees would shift to hit the pedals and my hand would stay there till her legs were wet.

Hic est enim calix sanguinis mei, the priest says, which shall be shed for you and for all men for the remission of sins. He raises the battered cup to the sunlight. Rose's notes would falter and her body would shudder slightly, a tiny missive I was coming to recognise. She would tell me to stop, but without conviction. Her eyes would fix on the manuscript as if the dots charted the rhythm of her breathing. She would only speak of it in musical terms. Moderato cantabile. The more profound her pleasure was, the less she referred to it. Afterwards I would play the same tune while she stood by the window and smoked. Music, I realised, was the way to keep Maisie's footsteps at bay. And Rose tried to disapprove, but her heart wasn't in it. Give over, Donal, she'd say, what would your father think? Till the day I took the dusty record from the pile of my mother's things in the attic upstairs.

It was Rachmaninov playing himself. When she came for her regular class I showed it to her and placed it on the phonograph. I put the needle down, turned up the volume gradually and his second concerto filled the room. What's this? she asked. Sit here and listen, I said, tapping the space on the couch beside me. I want to learn this. She sat beside me and let me take her hand, which was by now smaller than my own. She listened with her head back, let me unclasp one stocking, then the other. Stop it, Donal, she said when I undid the buttons of her blouse, but again her heart wasn't in it. Her hand played with my hair, my mouth and then in a moment of surrender eased me down on to the carpet. The playing was impossibly good and I wondered whether Maisie would notice the orchestral bits or hear our ever-more impassioned breathing but gradually the concerto seemed to fill the house, to echo round the promenade, beyond the railings and out over the Irish Sea.

O res mirabilis. I remember Mouse's voice echoing round the arches of the church on the windy hill. And the priest now turns to give the wafer to both of his muscular altar-boys, to the Garda Civil who walk forwards as meek as any line of schoolgirls while the Moroccan still whacks the stays of the tower that holds him. The wind blows in one last gust with hardly enough breath to shift the Virgin, sending eddies of sand round my ankles, and I know the moment has passed and I'm still standing.

Afterwards we lay in one another's arms and the record had got stuck in a groove, playing the same three notes over and over again. And that's it, Donal, she said. That in the end is where it all leads to. All what? I asked her. Everything, she said, every word, every hope, every glance across a crowded room, the whole damn thing all leads up to that. And that's your lesson for today. I reached out to bang the phonograph, wondering what she meant, when the door opened and I saw Maisie standing in the wedge of dust-coloured light.

The carpet, she said.

What about the carpet? I asked.

I need to do the carpet, she said.

Rose's stockings were hanging from the side of the couch, behind which she lay, her face deep crimson, mouth closed to prevent an explosion of laughter.

Rose got wet, I said, to explain the stockings.

It's not raining, said Maisie.

From the sea, I said.

The carpet, she said again, closing the door.

Maisie was simple, but not that simple. I turned to Rose and saw that all urge to laugh was gone.

I better go, she said. She stood quickly, pulled her stockings over her feet.

Don't worry, I said to her.

It's not her, she said. It's your father.

She won't tell, I said to her.

She will. Some day, she said.

Let her, I said.

You're a kid, she said, you don't understand.

But she didn't tell, whether because of an innate simplicity or sense of decorum I would never know. I sat at tea that evening waiting for the words to blurt out of her, some remark about the mythical rain, her being wet again with stockings undone, but she served us in silence, then returned to the book she had open by the range.

Rose, however, took it to heart. The thought of my father knowing struck her with an almost scriptural force. The next week she listened to me play with a sternness that would have done any country schoolteacher proud. When I walked her back to the station she talked. I'm sorry, she said, I shouldn't have let you. I should have had more sense. I wouldn't have let you stop me, I said. It's my fault, she said, I should have left long ago. No, I said, it's not your fault. Blame the music. So it's Rachmaninov's fault then, she said, smiling wryly. I love you, Rose, I said, surprised at how easily the words slipped out. You don't, she said, and I'm going to stop teaching you. You can't, I told her. I can, she said, and I have to. What will you tell my father? The truth, she said.

The truth, I thought. The truth about the roses on her   **49** dress and the way her hair spread out on the carpet. What is the truth? I asked her. The truth, she said, is that you're a bold boy and I'm a hussy. And I'm the one who should have known better. But you can't stop coming, I told her. Why can't I? she asked. Because you won't tell him, I said.

And that was the truth. We came to the station then but she drew me on, through the back streets till we came to the church. Come inside, she told me. So we walked into the draughty hall. I watched her sit in the back row beneath a picture of the Garden of Gethsemane. Sit down beside me, she said. I obeyed her and we both looked up at the altar. Now tell Him you're sorry. I'm not, I told her. How come I am? she asked me. Maybe you're sorry enough for both of us, I said, and she laughed. We sat in silence for a while. I presumed what she was doing was asking for forgiveness. After a time I let my hand touch her leg. She smacked it away, but laughed again. We're not getting very far, are we? I asked. She shook her head and blessed herself.

Pater noster, qui es in caelis, the priest says, facing the spatters of blood on the monastery wall. I asked her outside whether God had spoken to her. She told me that indeed He had. But the burden of the conversation she never shared with me. I was to discover it at next week's lesson. She listened to me play with the same abstracted air as on her first day. You could at least talk to me, Rose, I said, wrapping up the piece. That's true, Donal, she said, then patted my hair and left without a further word. I followed her down the promenade, at about twenty yards behind. She would turn, see me following, wave me away, then walk on again. The next week followed a similar pattern.

So God expressed Himself as always, through silences. I came to accept them after a while, came to enjoy them, even: the pregnant silence between phrases of music, the occasional hush of her voice and now and then, as before, but infinitely more nostalgic, the feel of her hands on mine when she came to correct me. We came to relish our status as sinners, the melancholy of the truly damned.

The winter came on and the rains with it and the gabardine coat she wore was wet more often than not. Her hair hung around her face in moist curls. I progressed to Debussy, and the fractured harmonies reinforced my sense of exile. We had banished ourselves from each other, from that intimate contact and need that after a time was like a dream, so distant it seemed. She became Rose, my piano teacher, which was what she was after all. There was a pain in the blunt reality of this fact but after a time I must have grown up, for I began to forget the pain too. I could open the door and welcome her, say, Hello, Rose; say, Maisie, what time is Rose due, without the world turning somersaults between the phrases.

Then one afternoon, the lesson ended, I walked her to the door and said, See you, Rose, next week.

You won't, she said, and my heart skipped a beat.

What do you mean I won't? I asked her.

You'll see me at the weekend, she says. Your father's asked me.

Asked you what? I said.

To come out here. For a picnic.

I stared at her and wondered why I had to keep myself from shaking.

And you said yes.

I did. Thought it would be nice. The three of us.

She walked towards the promenade then, leaving the door open, holding her music case up to shield her face from the rain.

I sat with him at teatime and waited for him to mention it. He didn't, so the silence that seemed the natural state of things continued. I sat the next night and again waited. Again he didn't, so I asked.

Rose is coming out, I said to him, more a statement than a question.

She told you? he muttered, reading as he ate.

For a picnic, she said.

Yes, he said. I thought it would be nice. The three of us.

He was repeating her phrases, but the words seemed foreign. I wondered then had she asked him.

We don't spend enough time together.

You and Rose? I asked.

No, he said. You, me, the three of us.

Why didn't you tell me? I asked him.

I was about to, he said.

When I asked you?

More or less.

I got up, cleaned my plate and walked outside. The sun was perched over the low tide like a beached whale. The light was beautiful and bilious. I wondered what conversation had led to that conversation and how many of them there had been. I tried to picture the three of us, napkin spread with scones between us, sipping tea in the Wicklow Hills. I wondered whose silences would be the most severe: mine, his or hers.

Mine were, in the end. We trudged through the Devil's Glen, me holding the hamper, both of them ahead of me like Mouse's vision of a courting couple. I felt churlish, even ridiculous in my silences but could think of nothing to say. That she had changed I could notice. From the girl who came to our door five years ago she had become a woman. She walked the way a woman walked, took her shoes off the way a woman would, planting her feet square in the damp grass, catching his arm when she stumbled, smoothing the linen cloth over the rock we had chosen to eat on with an almost maternal air. She expected something, a new stage in her life; the girl she had been on the piano stool now wanted something, something vague and undefined, but something very close to me. And whatever it was, it felt to me obscene.

I lay with my head in the grass, staring at the parting clouds, trying to define this obscenity. He was relating some story about a reception for the German ambassador. Donal, you're too quiet, she said. I know, I said, I'm sorry, and raised my head when he came to the punchline and attempted to laugh. But the laugh wouldn't come.

We both stood at the train when the day was over and watched her depart. He talked and I maintained my silence. About the day, the way it went, how we should do these things more often. We should, I lied, then walked in silence with him home.

Ite, Missa est, the priest says, and the ceremony is ended. But we can't take him at his word and go yet, we have to wait till he washes and wraps his cruets, till the altar-boys grab the makeshift altar and march ahead of him to the ruins of the monastery door. He'll return next week in the battered truck with his black case and the miracles inside. Then our guards walk round in a lazy swagger and click their tongues against their teeth as they would to cattle and we take it as a signal to move. We are marched towards the cool of the hard shadows by the monastery wall, through the low arch and down the steps. The sun comes in great shafts through the cellar windows, which move from left to right throughout the day. We'll shift around the straw-covered floor as it does, crowding into the shadows, the only diversion whatever happens in the square outside.

The thin boy from Seville takes his place by the window and stares at the blood-spattered wall. You'll take my place, *Irlandés,* when the time comes. We look like each other, no? I tell him we do, and that I will. Then I'll go to Ireland and meet your sister. I tell him I have to disappoint him about the sister. Ah, he says, and smiles, as if it had been a possibility after all. Then maybe I stay here. Maybe, I tell him, that is the only viable option. So when they come to shoot me, *Irlandés,* you will hold my hand? I tell him that if I hold his hand, the likelihood is I will be shot too. So we go together, he says, like I should have gone with Frederick?

He is in our cell because he joined, incongruously for a Spaniard, the Abraham Lincoln battalion. The lover of a Boston student, he signed up with him in Paris and they made their way to Madrid. Frederick was hit by a Red Cross truck two miles behind the lines, denying both of them the glorious demise they had imagined.

How would you have gone with Frederick? I ask him, but before he can tell me yet again we're diverted by the sounds outside. Here we go, Pat, the Welshman says, and takes his pew at the ledge by the window. They lead a line of shoeless figures from the shadows into the hot sun. One of them breaks and runs and the Moroccan in the box-tower decides to put his gun to better use. He aims and fires twice and the figure falls, a dark shadow on the whitened ground, a darker stain gradually spreading around it. The others shuffle forwards with eerie obedience and form a line by the blood-spattered wall. The guards make an untidy half-circle, raise their rifles and create an intermittent staccato like a badly played kettle-drum till the line has become a crumpled heap.

Inside we say nothing for a while. Then Antonio beside me tugs at my belt. You'll think of me, *Irlandés,* when they shoot me? I tell him that if they shoot him, they will shoot all of us, and that if they shot all of us, diplomatic incidents would ensue. He shakes his head, smiling wryly. No, he says, they take the one Spaniard from the cell and shoot him, like a dog. I shake my head, knowing that I'm wrong. And when they shoot me, he says, I want you to think of me. I assure him I think of him hourly. No, he says, I want you to read this and think of me. He takes a crumpled paper from his pocket and holds it to the light. From Frederick, he says, and asks me to read.

It is a yellowing scrap, torn from a book. I read.

> Because I could not stop for death—
> He kindly stopped for me—
> The carriage held but just ourselves—
> And immortality.

He waits for more but the page is torn and at the rough edges the words are indecipherable. What does it mean? he asks. I tell him it is a poetic meditation on the theme of death, quite at odds with the shabby ceremonials outside. But beautiful, no? Beautiful indeed, I tell him, but useless. Frederick had a use for it, he says. He said his soul was in the words. And if you read it when they shoot me, mine will be in them too.

I look at his dark eyes by the barred window and my own feel wet. Because he accepts it so readily, I can only believe it will happen. So I promise him I'll read it if they come to shoot him, if they haven't shot me first. He rewards me with a smile.

The gun was to blame. It hinted at a past of his I'd never seen, at possibilities I dared not think of. The piano lost its frisson for me, though the lessons kept on, like the memory of movement in a limb that has been severed. I took the gun walking with Mouse along the tracks round the Head, laying bullets from the chamber on the metal struts and waiting till a train came by to explode them. I took to shooting salmon in the river by the harbour, in midair as they leapt up the weir, flashes of silver which would explode when hit in a stripe of red. The nightlines had become a memory as well by then and this mode of fishing would have to suffice. I sat on the peak of the Head one afternoon with the town below me and the sprawl of the city beyond. I put one bullet in the chamber, spun it, then stuck the barrel in my ear and listened to the sound of the trigger as I pulled. A greasy click, slow, like the operation of a giant wheel as the chamber moved and then I knew either an explosion of sound and the final silence or a further click. I heard the hammer hit home and then a silence did descend, the clouds moved in quiet glory over Djouce mountain, the sun came through in a many-fingered burst and I relished my escape. It was a version of death, a peace beyond anything life could throw at me. I tried again with Mouse, in the old mill behind the sewage plant. Here, I

56

told him, a game of chance, and showed him how I put the single bullet in the chamber, spun it with the palm of one hand and shoved the barrel in my ear. Stop it, Dony, he said. Why? I asked him. Give me one reason why. I waited for a reason and when he had none squeezed the trigger. He hit the gun from my hand as I did so and it exploded, sending the bullet into the watertower of the sewage plant behind. We watched a stream of amber-coloured liquid squirt from the tower. There's your reason, he said.

It was an escape though, of another kind. The liquid fell, silently, in a long arc and formed a puddle at our feet. Mouse was shouting at me, his mouth opening and closing, though no sound came out. Then he hit me in the face and I could hear again. Could have been you, he said, you fucking nut. That stream of piss, I said. Yeah, he said, and turned away, it could have been you.

I kept it with me, though, tucked into the pocket of a gabardine coat I developed the habit of wearing. I took the train to Dublin, to a meeting of the Republican Congress in Rathmines Town Hall. I heard grizzled old veterans of his war rail against the Free State, talk about the betrayal of just about everything, including the Republic and the working class. "I knew your father" became a kind of refrain to me, expressed with a hint of regret and disapproval and a large dollop of suspicion about my presence there. He had put his name to several publications on the danger of the growing tide of anarchy, De Valera's betrayal of the principles of the Treaty and the rising communist menace. I watched him speak in the Royal Dublin Society on the virtues of the corporate state. I stood in the background while they drove a flock of goats through the august premises, twenty through each door, and I could see from the back his expression as a   **57** large horned monster leapt the podium. Cries of Blueshirt! and Fascist! and scum of all description echoed round the hall as the meeting broke up in chaos and my last glimpse was of him, tall, statuesque, his bearded mouth still moving soundlessly amidst the mayhem.

I took the train home, wondering did he know I had been there. I found him standing in the kitchen, a glass of whiskey in his hand. You were there, he said, I saw you near the back. It was a public gathering, I said. What happened, he asked, to the right to disagree? I don't want to argue, I said. Do, he said, tell me what they would have replied if they hadn't taken recourse to a herd of goats. Don't worry about it, I said. You kept your dignity intact. What does that mean? he asked. It means, I said, you expounded your Fascist drivel with all the decorum of a gentleman. Where did you learn those words? he asked; those aren't your words. I'll make them mine, I said. They're teaching you to hate me, he said. And who is they? I asked. Those latter-day Republicans, he said, those corner-boys and counter-jumpers, the ones who've made a career out of hating. I don't hate you, I said, to myself as much as to him. Then I wondered had I told a lie, or at best a half-truth. He must have wondered too, for he finished his whiskey and walked towards the kitchen door.

A key rattles in the metal lock and the barred door opens. A triangle of light comes in and they come in with it in their triangular hats. The Spaniard turns his face to the shadows but it is me they point at. I stand and approach the tilted gun-muzzle and the fear that has run through everyone shifts in me like a dulled ulcer.

I walk between them down the long corridor with its

peeling parabola of white. They gesture the way with their hands, quite without suspicion or hate, as if both seem pointless now that it is all over. We pass a plaster-cast statue of Christ in the wall. Both the hands are broken and the guard nearest me turns to me and grins. He mutters in a dialect I can't fathom and I smile back to show I understand. We come to a door which they both reach to open, then one steps back to let the other do so and they usher me inside. We pass through a room without windows, with a plain wooden desk and a water bucket with a dull liquid inside it. One sits by the desk, the other stands by the bucket and gestures me towards the door beyond.

I open the door and see an oak table and a silver cigarette case, a carafe of water and diamond-cut glasses. There is a man sitting at the table, German, his uniform bearing the insignia of the Abwehr, with a sheaf of papers in his hand. His skin is fair, as unused to the sun as mine is. After a space of seconds he says, Please close the door.

I obey. The room has church-like windows with a fan revolving in the ceiling.

Gore, he says, Donal Gore.

I nod, then when he stays silent, I say, That's me.

The question is, I suppose, what is one of your nationality doing here?

Waiting, I say.

Or should I rephrase it, he says. How did one of your nationality get here?

There is another bucket near the wall, dark water inside, a rag floating in it, stained with crimson.

I volunteered, I say.

Why?

Do I have to give an account of myself?

He looks up, for the first time. Green eyes and sandy hair, a freckled sunburnt face and a mouth that seems amused at nothing in particular.

No, he says, in precise Oxford tones, but it would be simpler if you did.

Why? I ask him.

You've seen what happens in the square outside. If you co-operate, it could be to your advantage.

And if I don't?

He shrugs, then lights a cigarette and reads from the sheaf of papers.

You were born into a middle-class Irish family, your mother died when you were six, your father was a minister in the Free State government.

He inhales, looking at a paper in front of him.

Your first encounter with politics was with the Republican Congress in Dublin. He exhales, and raises two pale eyebrows.

So, he says. You tell me. What brought you here?

He was eating bacon from the breakfast Maisie had prepared for him when I said I was going and the strings of bacon stuck between his teeth and he had to pause between his sentences to pick out the bacon with a sharpened match so his words were even less frequent than normal. You are leaving, he said, because you hate me, not because of any nebulous political ideas. And though it might have been true, I said it wasn't. And you think you hate me because of her, but in fact you hate me because I am simply me, your father. Please, he said, as I moved to leave, get your hatreds in perspective, otherwise you'll never—and he stopped there, as if he couldn't finish. Never what? I asked. But he said nothing else, so I went.

The cigarette is nearing its end. The German lets the ash fall from his lip to the surface of the oak table in front of him.

Representations, he says, have been made on your behalf. You would be most unwise to ignore them.

By whom? I ask.

I don't know, and frankly, I don't care. So what brought you here?

My father, I say.

Your father brought you here? He smiles.

No. He's tried to arrange—

Ah. Your father has made the representations? Perhaps. As I told you, I neither know nor care. My function is simply to get some answers to some simple questions.

For instance?

If I must repeat myself, what brought you here?

She had come the night before with her music case under her arm—out of habit, I assumed, since we had long given up all pretext of lessons. Let me be the first to congratulate you, I said, aware that he could see us from the living-room window, walking the length of the promenade. The evening sky was immaculate, the sea was serene, only disturbed by the movement of paddle-boats around the Head. You can't blame me, she said, you can't take that tone. What tone is that, Rose? I asked her. I don't expect you to understand, she said; I don't want to talk about it. So what can we talk about? I asked her. You, she said. You'll kill him if you go. So, I said, maybe there is a reason to my going after all. How did you get like this? she asked. I don't know, I said. Maybe the sins of fathers are visited on their sons. He is a good man, she said, better than you've ever given him credit for. Better than you'll ever know if you go like this. So where should I stay, Rose? I asked her. In the bedroom next to yours? He asked me, she said, he asked me to consider his affection for me. He finds it difficult to say such things; I was touched, I said I would and you're going to tell me that's a crime. All I've said is my congratulations, I told her. Donal, she said, and she grabbed me and pushed my shoulderblades against the promenade railings, I'm begging you, don't do this to him. So it's him it's being done to, I said. All right, she said, and took a breath. Don't do it to me, then. I'm not doing it to you, I said.

She was wearing a peach-coloured dress underneath her gabardine. Her blonde hair was piled on her head in a way that was new to me. She laid her chin on my shoulder and stared out at the sea. I have a feeling, she said. A premonition. Of what? I asked. Something dreadful. Something worse than dreadful. If you go. I can't stay, Rose, I said, as softly as I could. You know that. Let me leave, then, she said. I'll get out of your lives. It'll be as if you never saw me. The thing is, Rose, I said, it can never be that. It can't? she said. Then go and be damned. 'Cause you will be.

I volunteered, I tell him, I took the course of action most likely to wound my father. I became the person he was most likely to fear, despise, to loathe. I wanted to quench for ever the last embers of speech between us. I joined the Republican movement he had abandoned, espoused whatever politics would fill him with terror. I walked into Liberty Hall by the Liffey in Dublin on an April morning and stood in a queue with a line of other lost souls and when my time came I wrote my name down. So what brought me here was a series of accidents, beginning with the accident of birth, a childhood spent on the promenade in Bray, a holiday town not a stone's throw from Dublin, a slender talent for music at an early age, the discovery of certain sentimental harmonies in the company of a woman who was to become my stepmother. And, while we are at it, nightlines.

Nightlines? he queries, a smile playing on his thin lips.

Nightlines, I say, a practise common in the South of Ireland. Two metal rods with a line of hooks strung between them, to be jammed in the sand at low tide, the hooks skewered with rag or lugworms, take your pick, then left to simmer as the ocean passes over them until morning.

And in the morning? he asks. His smile has broadened.

In the morning the tide, following a logic known only to itself, makes an orderly retreat, leaving a ray, a plaice, a pollock or, if you're lucky, a salmon bass swinging from the hooks. This practise to be indulged in at arbitrary intervals with a familiar who may relish the sense of relative peace it brings, the main pleasure, I might add, being in the silence brought about by the absence of the need for speech.

Is that all? he asks.

No, I say. Lest I misrepresent the pleasures of this ritual, it should be stressed that the actual catch is ancillary to the process. The evening walk with the hooks swinging between 63 both participants is without doubt the high point. The morning's catch is an afterthought, a by-product, often-times a let-down.

I think I understand, he says.

No, I say, you don't. Neither for that matter do I. But if representations have been made on my behalf by my father, I will regretfully have to decline them.

What precisely do you mean by that?

It means, I say, I won't accept his patronage. Or yours. Whatever sordid arrangement he came to with your superiors is nothing to do with me. Now, if you'll excuse me.

I stand. He stands too. He says certainly, then floors me with a straight right from the shoulder, western style. I feel a mouthful of knuckles, an exploding lip, and find my head crashing off the bucket on the floor. It wobbles, then falls, spilling stale blood and water over my chest.

He walks round the oak table and stretches down a hand. I take it.

You must excuse me also, he says. It is after all the least that is expected of me.

He pulls me upwards. He smiles, pats my cheek, then turns me towards the door.

Let's talk again tomorrow, he says.

There is a cry I recognise as they walk me back down the peeling corridor. I hold my sleeve to my lips to stem whatever blood is coming from them. They turn the key in the barred door then and push me back inside the room. Every figure there is hunched by the windows, dark against the streaming light. I hear the cry again like the strangled gull my father had inadvertently imitated when he ran from the fishing lines. I walk across the straw-covered floor and peer above their shoulders. I see Antonio standing by the wall, head tilted backwards at a strange angle, staring at the sky. Three Moroccans raise their rifles nonchalantly and fire at random while his figure jerks, an odd dance to the rhythm of their bullets. He spins several times, face to the wall, then face to us, and falls.

There's silence in the room. The Welshman coughs then, a spasm, born out of years on some coalface. The boy from Turin mutters a prayer. The Germans withdraw from the window and sit back in the straw, drawing their long knees towards their chins. I take the scrap of paper he gave me from my pocket. I am several seconds and maybe an eternity too late since his blood has spread a pool as large again around his body, but I read it anyway. *Because I could not stop for death—He kindly stopped for me.*

They rough you up, Pat?

The Welshman talks between wheezes. I remember my split lip and for a moment am glad of it.

A little, I say.

And what did they want?

Wanted to know what brought me here, I tell him.

You find out anything?

Like what?

What's going to happen to us.

I shake my head to intimate infinite possibilities, then turn back to the window.

When did they come for him? I ask.

Just before you came in.

He coughs again, then stares at me.

You know something, don't you, Pat.

What could I know? I ask him.

You tell me.

———

In the night his shadow edges over to my bed, invisible hands are laid upon my shoulder and his voice whispers, You cannot sleep, *Irlandés,* like me, neither. His ghostly syntax is as misplaced as ever. I turn, about to brush him off, but see nothing there. Soft moonlight coming through each window and the figures huddled in the straw around the walls. It comes to me suddenly, with an odd, perfect clarity, that all of us could die here. Our release would be too troublesome, and once released we would have tales to tell. The Welshman snoring, his broken nose pointing towards the ceiling, the two Germans, their hair indistinguishable from the straw, the Jewish boy from Turin, all beyond the help of ordinary discourse. I think of us joining that realm below the waves and fall asleep dreaming of the Abwehr officer plucking us from a row of hooks from which we swing, gently, in the morning light.

And I am called to him next morning. The same two guards, through the triangle of the early morning light, walking me with the same brutal insouciance through the vaulted tomb. The German sits and smokes, questions as before. Nothing will do for him but some answers, so I reply, inventing a past that might satisfy him. Yesterday's outburst was just that, an outburst, I tell him. But what you want is the truth. The word seems to satisfy him and he nods. How does the son of an Irish reactionary find himself in Republican Spain?

My father's world, I tell him, was an unfinished one. I joined the Republican movement to bring it to some conclusion. His revolt had been stillborn, dissipating its energies in the nonsense of a civil war. The State resulting from it was one of paralysis, echoed in himself. I became his nemesis, his alter ego, took up the gun he'd dropped and made it my own. The divisions in Europe echoed ours, or was it the other way round, I forget now, but it seemed important at the time to make them my own. So here I am.

And what now? he asks.

What about now? I reply.

Where do your sympathies lie?

Where they always did, I say. With the Republic.

Irish or Spanish?

Both, I say.

But the one you said is stillborn and the other you know is finished.

I am Irish, I say. I live in realms of pure possibility.

Representations have been made, he says, and I can only act on them under certain conditions.

Who made these representations? I ask.

To repeat myself, that is irrelevant. I can only act on them under certain conditions.

What conditions are they? I ask.

We have contacts with some members of your movement. We need to expand them.

You want me to collaborate?

Phrase it as you want. To quote your movement, England's difficulty is Ireland's opportunity.

And what precisely is England's difficulty?

That remains to be seen.

My father, I tell him, would be most unhappy with this turn of events.

Why?

Look at it through his eyes, I say. He arranges for diplomatic pressure to be exerted to free his wayward son. His son will only be freed on conditions that make him more wayward.

Everything has to be paid for.

Perhaps, I tell him, but my answer will always be no.

Why? he asks.

Because, I think, he gave me life once and I won't accept the same gift twice.

Because, I tell him, what you propose is unthinkable.

For myself I don't give a damn, he says, and the slang comes out oddly from his lips. My job is to file a report. But you are being more stupid than even I could have thought possible.

Why? I ask him.

Your time here has run out. They will erase this place together with all memory of it. You'll be shot.

That will have the virtue, I tell him, of keeping things simple.

You like simplicity? he asks.

Yes, I tell him. I feel my hands sweating, underneath my bluster. And it would be simpler not to change my mind.

I stand. I expect a knuckleful in the mouth again, and am almost disappointed when it doesn't come. He stands too and bends his head, a quick, odd little bow.

Thank you, he says. You have made my job easier. My report shall be brief. And simple.

He smiles as if waiting for me to change my mind. And I would, if I could feel something, some premonition of the world having changed, but there is nothing there, merely the sweat running down my fingers and down my forehead now. And I wonder is this fear that has not yet reached me. He snaps his fingers and the guards come to the door. They walk me back the same corridor and I hear cries once more. I am pushed inside to see the Welshman

being dragged, barrel-chested and screaming, from a

mound of flailing straw. Three guards around him, and seven more pressing the others to the wall.

I'm an Englishman, he screams, in his thick Welsh vowels. Write that down, you bastards. I move towards him and feel a rifle-butt against my split lip and hit the straw beneath me. The three get him through the door and the others then follow with a careless swagger.

The German boys stand by the wall and a dark stain spreads down the trousers of one of them. The Turin boy moans from his hide of straw. No one can bring themselves to move to the window. We hear the outer door clang and his screaming stops. We can hear the mutter of obscenities through his clenched teeth and then the sound of dragging pebbles as they move him to the wall and after a moment's silence, the dull thud of shots. As staccato as before, but more of them.

When we can engender the will to get to the window, it is over. He is being dragged by both feet to a waiting truck, his barrel chest still streaming, leaving a trail of blood behind him. The truck shudders as its engine ticks over, waiting for the lines of Spaniards being led to the spot on the wall he has vacated.

There is a certain dignity, the German with the dry trousers says, in being shot on one's own.

That night, there were no dreams. I counted fish on an imaginary line to will myself to sleep and when it eventually came, it was blank, like God's silence. I awoke with the first light and the knowledge that when they came for me it would not be to ask questions. The mound of hay on which the German youths slept now stank of disengaged bowels. But they were silent as oxen in their stalls, as if the

69

world had ended. I lay there watching the light turn the straw to gold and when it was all ablaze I heard the feet.

They came with intent, nailed boots striking off the flagstones outside. The door opened and the room was full of them, three to keep the others in place and three to drag me. The first three were redundant since rigor mortis had already touched those in the straw and they stayed, apparently sleeping. The others pulled me in one movement and dragged me, my feet scraping off the floor. I tried to help them and walk but all life had gone from my muscles and any moisture in my mouth had retreated to the pit of my stomach. *Because I could not stop for death,* I thought, but could not remember what followed. They pulled me through to the arches and behind me I heard the door clanging shut. I closed my eyes: I didn't want to face the blinding sunlight, the square, the reddened wall. I had told myself that when it came I would be calm, retain whatever dignity was left to me. And now that it had come I had no alternative but calm, that awful silence I had always suspected lay behind it all, for my lips moved and no sound came out. I would have screamed had it been possible but nothing could move, shift or whisper in this pit my body had become. I was inert and howling inside it but outside all else was dumb. Then I realised we had not turned. What should have been the crunch of pebbles beneath their feet was still their boots on the flagstones; what should have been the sun bleaching the red behind my closed eyelids was still dark. I let my eyelids open slowly, saw the curved, vaulted ceiling coming to me and away. Then another door. They have taken a different route, I thought, to another end of the square; and two of them opened the door and I saw open countryside outside. The

German standing there, bleached by the light, pale leather gloves on his hands, an open-topped car behind him. Come with me, Irish, he said, whether you like it or not.

The hands let go. I swayed on my numb feet. *He kindly stopped for me,* I remembered.

We drive through the outskirts, factories reduced to rubble, bomb craters filled with water, lines of people walking in both directions as if the destination doesn't matter. His white scarf blows in the wind and the kid gloves play non-chalantly at the wheel, one hand continuously on the horn. He talks of how they'll make the world a rubbish-tip, cut through cities like a cleansing wind, how he would care if his uniform allowed him. He was a physicist, he tells me, worked in Leipzig with Heisenberg on the uncertainty principle. He relates to me the bones of quantum physics, says how Einstein claimed God does not play dice with the universe then tells me how he discovered God does nothing else. His father was Prussian, an officer, rooted in the civi-lised brutalities of the Wehrmacht. Perturbed by the more pervasive brutalities of the Reich, he was foolish enough to express his feelings and now worked as a sub-postmaster in Silesia. Both of his brothers joined the Waffen SS, and he had chosen to hide himself in the bureaucratic niceties of the Abwehr. I ask him the connection between that and the uncertainty principle and he tells me to look around me.

Lorries full of returning loyalists are passing us from the north and the legs of a child jut out behind a mound of rubble.

I was an indifferent mathematician, he tells me, more interested in metaphors than equations. And quantum the-ory was as apt a metaphor as any for what I saw around me.

I have no taste for brutalities but a certain aptitude for interrogation. I listen, I ask the pertinent question after the teeth have been extracted by others, I find civility works wonders. My brief, if you must know, was to question those members of your brigade whose sympathies may be uncertain. You fell into that category by reason of your movement's approaches to the Reich. You knew about this?

I shake my head.

You have some argument with Britain?

I shake my head again.

Then certain of your compatriots do. Whether you do or don't, frankly, I couldn't give a damn. That's how you say it?

As good a way as any, I tell him.

You will be contacted in Dublin by persons possibly unknown to you. Whether or not you act upon these contacts is no concern of mine.

He drives in silence for a while.

Frankly, my dear, I don't give a damn.

He smiles. It's from a film they made while you were inside. Clark Gable, walking down the staircase. Vivien Leigh, walking up. *Gone with the Wind.* See it, when you get the chance.

We are bumping across a makeshift bridge over the Ebro, the ruins of the aqueduct to our left. Beyond it, miles of broken farmland, as far as the eye can see.

In fact, he continues, you would have been released either way. Representations have been made on your behalf.

He is repeating himself, I tell him.

OK. But be so kind as to repeat to me the burden of
what I've told you.

You studied at the University of Leipzig with Heidegger.

Heisenberg. Heidegger holds the chair of philosophy at Freiburg. But that was not my question. About your movement.

They have had certain contacts with the Reich.

Yes. And on your return, you are to resume your contacts with your former comrades. In time you will be approached by persons unknown.

Should I get out and walk? I ask him.

Yes, if you wish to be a martyr and an idiot.

Then stop the car.

He screeches to a halt. The landscape is lost in a cloud of dust and my head crashes off the windscreen.

Be my guest.

A trickle of blood runs down my nose. I feel for the door handle, push it down and stagger outside. He looks at me with amused contempt. I wipe my nose and smile and thank him and walk forwards. As the dust clears I see the ruins of a farmhouse in the distance, the thin line of refugees starting again. To the left of my feet is what must have once been an irrigation ditch, now filled with bloated cattle. I walk forwards. I attempt to calculate the walk to Barcelona and guess it at fourteen days. After a time I hear the Hispano-Suiza purring behind me.

Irish, he calls.

Hans, I answer. The car draws alongside.

Am I to take it you won't act upon my brief?

Yes, I tell him.

Then please accept my hospitality.

I stop, wipe the blood again and look at him, his face still wreathed in the same smile.

This is no time for heroics, my friend.

I turn again and walk on, knowing the car will follow. And after a time it does.

You heard what I said?

Which part?

All of them.

I heard the lot, I tell him. And while not wishing to offend you, I think I might enjoy the walk.

The smile diminishes somewhat.

You do offend me.

Then please accept my apologies.

I bend my head, to signal my regret, then walk on. I hear silence behind me for a time, then the engine roars and he passes me in a cloud of dust.

The cattle by the ditch are long-horned, their ribs showing through their cases of skin. Their stench is overpowering. I walk on, my hand over my face, and slowly, ever so slowly, the line of figures comes closer. A dozen men in front, like a bedraggled bunch of navvies, and behind them women and children. We pass, without exchanging a glance. The ruins come closer and I see instead of a farmhouse, the remains of a hamlet, smoke rising out of a bare chimney unsupported by walls. The sun in time congeals the blood on my face, then the sweat from my forehead makes it flow again. I can see a table now beneath the chimney, an open fire with scattered motorcycles round it. Glinting in the sunlight, a phalanx of three-cornered hats. They turn as I approach, to watch the sole figure walking in their direction. The smell of charcoal drifts towards me, mixed with a hint of pork. I can see a suckling pig roasting on a spike, a young boy turning it. A figure in torn khaki tied to a broken column, the head bent down at an unnatural angle. Two of the three-cornered hats rise. They walk towards me, casting tiny shadows, thumbs stuck in their ammunition belts. I follow the only course open to me and walk on.

Buenos días, I mutter, with what I hope is a hint of dialect, and they step aside to let me walk between them. I keep an even pace, down the centre of the track, then hear their footsteps close and congeal behind me. I think it unwise to turn, but hesitate for a moment, then feel my feet kicked from beneath me.

I smile as I hit the dirt, try to raise my hands in a supplicant manner when they grab them, flip me over and drag me face down towards the table. I can see the figure in khaki still motionless, tied to the broken column. They dump me by the burning embers, beneath the suckling pig on its spike, and the fat leaps from its browning skin to the skin of my face. One of them plants a boot in my shoulders. I attempt to comprehend their talk as the weight crushes my chest into the pebbles. The breath squeezes out of me slowly and one of them rises, takes a knife from his belt and cuts off the roasted flesh in strips. He turns the spike slowly, shifting the carcass on its axis, and chews as he mumbles instructions. The pressure on my back eases and the hands above me drag me over to the column. The kid in khaki with his neck bent strangely can't be more than fifteen. His lips are blue and the rope that jams his neck to the sandstone column has plenty to spare. They wrap it around mine so my cheek touches his, then tighten it with a perfunctory jerk. I breathe in long strangled gasps, and each struggle to breathe better causes the rope to tighten more. I can see spots in front of my eyes, the figures in the three-cornered hats, like blurred puppets in the sun, sitting by the table, bringing pigmeat to their mouths. They mutter as they eat and it seems to be about everyday things. Then I close my eyes, feel the blood sink to my bowels and hear a familiar sound: the even purring of the Hispano-Suiza. It comes closer; I open my eyes and see a haze of white. I hear the engine sputter into silence, the door open and his voice, in screaming Castilian, thick now with a German accent. He calls them sons of the leavings of whores and one of them walks towards me, cuts the rope with a knife that smells of pork gristle. My head flops downwards, almost on to the blade, and a pair of hands lifts me till my face is even with the patent-leather hat. Then the hands on my neck are replaced by ones covered in soft pigskin and he carries me over to the open door of the car.

You are an idiot, Irish, he says almost wistfully as he eases me inside. His gloves run along my neck where the rope burned it. He closes the door, takes the driver's seat and starts the engine, reverses suddenly so the high boot strikes the table, sending it cartwheeling in the dust, upending the bearers of the three-cornered hats. He guns it forwards then, and lurches off in the direction he came.

So, he says, you will accept my hospitality whether you like it or not.

We drove for three days and nights. Through towns covered with the dust of chalk, through a moonlit landscape of small broken farms. After a time, the swelling on my neck subsided and it was comfortable to talk. Until then, I listened. There is a price to pay for everything, he told me, rarely apparent at the time of the transaction, making its claim at the most unexpected moments. He himself had no doubt that his bill would come, but no longer understood the terms. Until then he was content to observe the demolition going on around him. He had become convinced from an early age that the greatest triumph of the human being was the most useless: the attempt to create meaning from a meaningless world; to create a moral system out of the random chaos of human affairs. The Reich's greatest triumph, he told me, was its recognition of chaos, of the arbitrary maelstrom that raged beneath the veneer of what we term civilisation. That recognition gave it power, a power it could use to create yet another absurdity: an amoral system based now upon an amoral premiss. So of the fact that he would one day pay, he had no doubt. His sole amusement lay in conjecture, of what form that payment would take.

I listened to him talk, watched his scarf blow in the wind, the pale glow of his hands on the wheel. There was a river behind him, following the road, then the ruins of a wall, an old broken millwheel, a courtyard with tables, the light of a *pensión* burning inside.

Can I call you by your name, Irish? he asked me softly.

Yes, I told him. You know it. Donal.

Donald, he said.

Donal, I told him. From the Gaelic.

We sat by a table and drank wine from earthen mugs.

So you are alive, Irish, he said. We must be thankful for small mercies.

You are my small mercy, I told him. And now I presume I must pay.

That seems to be the norm.

And I can only conjecture on what form this payment will take.

He ordered from a stout woman with a butcher's knife **77** who seemed to be proprietress, cook and waitress all at once.

You want to know the truth?

Is there one?

There is, and it is quite mundane. The truth is, I didn't have to take you. But now that you are with me, there are procedures. I must file a report, conjecture upon any possible use you may have, itemise your specific talents—

I am a moderate pianist, I told him.

And your contacts.

I have a friend, I told him, called Mouse.

You are right, he said, there is an absurdity at the heart of it. Even that I must itemise. You came here by way of the Republican movement.

By way of a faction of it, I told him.

Who are engaged in certain disturbances in Britain.

England's difficulty, I told him, is Ireland's opportunity.

That is your belief?

No, I quote.

Yes, I remember the phrase.

Would you believe me, I asked him, if I said I will be of no use to you?

I would, he said. But you must allow me the courtesy of procedures. Otherwise, I must leave you by the roadside.

You already did.

He nodded. You are right. I already did. But look what came of that.

The food came. Thin strips of pork, fried with rice. I ate slowly and swallowed with difficulty.

You said representations had been made, I asked him.

By whom?

He shrugged. You know someone in government circles?

My father.

Ah. Your father. He must love you.

He must.

You don't believe he does?

I don't think about it, I lied.

He slipped into conjecture then. The moon was sinking low over the river, throwing silver on the dried husk of the millwheel. He asked me to entertain the fiction that I could be of use and asked me to imagine what use that could be. I drew a picture of my homeland for him as a mandarin world where each statement had two meanings, its apparent meaning and its actual one. Foreigners, I told him, must approach us with circumspection, guile and an adamant refusal to believe things are as they seem. A naive acceptance of the surface of things would lead one to believe the island lay fifty miles off the coast of Britain, whereas its actual position could only be found with reference to medieval cartography, wherein the earth was flat and the boundaries to the known world lay somewhere to our west. My main use to him would be, I surmised, as interpreter, or to be more precise, diviner of the hidden facts, the hidden meanings, the hidden landscapes which lay behind the apparent ones.

Admirable, he said. I am not alone in my affection for metaphors.

Not at all, I assured him. The wine was going to my head. But there is one caveat.

What is that? he asked, his face flushed, and I hoped the wine was going to his head too.

My role as interpreter/diviner would itself be an apparent one.

Ah! he exclaimed, and I saw the wine was getting there, but you would still have provided the interpretive codes.

Perhaps, I said, but can that which is apparent be trusted to distinguish what is not?

We stagger from the tables towards the *pensión*. He supports me by the elbow, whispering that perhaps those distinctions will be made by people other than ourselves. I am by now tired of the whole conceit but can divine some hidden meaning in the clasp of his hand on my elbow. There is a wooden staircase leading to a small stone-walled room, two beds against opposite walls. He stands too close to me in the darkness, swaying slightly.

Scarlett, he says.

I ask him what he means.

An apparent name, for your apparent function.

Scarlett, I repeat.

Yes, he says. He walks slowly towards the bed to his left. You must see the motion picture.

What motion picture? I ask him.

Gone with the Wind, he says. And I shall be Rhett.

He sits there, staring at his boots, then looks from them to me.

Could you do me the honour, Irish.

I pull off one boot, then the other and place them by the wall. He lies slowly back, staring at the ceiling.

The scene on the staircase, Vivien Leigh walking upwards, Clark Gable walking down. Watch it, when you get home. Think of me.

There is a hint of self-pity in his voice which touches me. I lie on the other bed and feel sleep coming on in a rush. Then he speaks again, as if unwilling to let me depart.

You will think of me, Irish?

I tell him I will, then let the sleep take over.

The drive to Barcelona takes two more days. The city seems crushed, like a drugged patient afraid to let his eyes wander. The streets are empty of people, but for the posters of the General, which stare from every wall and lamppost, the Virgin, who stares from every church, and everywhere the three-cornered patent-leather hats. He drives through it to the port, where a statue of Columbus looks out on the Mediterranean. He has arranged my passage on a coal-tip, heading for Dublin. An Irish consular official is waiting by a black Ford, a sheaf of papers rustling in his hand, surrounded by a sea of triangular heads. My Abwehr deliverer walks through them with a contempt that is matched only by the distaste with which the consular official looks at me.

Gore, he says, Donal Gore.

I nod.

I knew your father, he mutters, ruffling through the papers. He looks at my ragged clothing.

How is he? I ask, but he doesn't reply.

Could you not have made yourself presentable?

I apologise. His accent is thick Cork.

Let's get it over with. He hands me a pen and papers to sign.

We walk in a phalanx towards the dock, the consular official from Cork ahead, behind him me and the German, behind us again the phalanx of triangular heads. Some odd ceremony of nations is taking place, the Cork official muttering to himself about scuts and layabouts and thooleramawns who should be left to rot in their own ordure, striding like an undersized zealot through yards of wooden warehouses, the German easily keeping pace with him, all of the Spaniards straining to keep up, their shoes shining even brighter than their patent-leather hats. We come to a mound of coal, the giant claw of a crane stretched over the brown water and beneath it a vessel that looks like an enlarged coal-scuttle. Three men in blackened vests are stretching a walkway to the pier.

He shakes my hand. His green eyes smile.

Scarlett, he says.

Rhett, I say. Did you believe a word I told you?

It needs interpretation, he says. Do not think badly of me.

I won't, I promise, and walk out on the ridged plank.

Tell your father, says the Corkman, Jeremiah Noonan sends his regards.

I will, I promise. His black eyes fall from mine to the water.

Are ye comin' or goin', shouts a Dublin voice from the boat. I look at the Spaniards, standing in a triangular phalanx behind them. I walk up the gangplank and step aboard.

We headed down the tip of Spain, past fleets of destroyers massing round Gibraltar. By Algeciras we saw a submarine slink below the waters like a giant seal. The coal-scuttle sent a constant trickle of black smoke into the air. When we hit the Atlantic it developed a sickening roll. I vomited for a day, then learnt sea-legs. Somewhere past Bilbao, the wizened stoker with the voice like grinding coke told me that Germany had invaded Poland. I looked out over the rolling seas and wondered would I think badly of him and wondered where his Hispano-Suiza was now. We pulled into Portsmouth for an afternoon and while the stokers looked for whores, I tried to find a cinema where I could see Vivien Leigh on the staircase going up, Clark Gable going down. Frankly, my dear, I don't give a damn.

II

I get off the boat in Dun Laoghaire and try not to feel familiar, which is difficult, seeing nothing has changed. The buses are the same green, smoke hangs in the air like a cloud of its own, the train that takes me out to Bray chugs with the same old languor. I tell myself that I have changed and all else hasn't, but even that isn't true. The old self folds round me like a comforting cloak. I want to see him, the old devil, I realise. The eucalyptus trees bend on the Vico Road and their scent comes through the window with the odour of tomcats. The bowling green is sodden outside the station and the long walk up to the terraces chills to the bone. The gates are hanging open, there is green moss and the accretions of rust over the ironwork. I look up at the house and see new lace curtains at the windows and realise that it's true, she must be there. So I walk on past all the railings and knock on the door and she answers.

Were you expecting me? I say, with as much quiet as I can muster.

Yes, she tells me.

Well, I say, here I am.

Good, she says.

Was he expecting me too?

In a way.

Her odd reply throws me for a moment. I can't bring myself to walk inside, nor can she, it seems, bring herself to ask me in. I throw my eyes up to hers and see hers fall away, searching for the spot I had been staring at on the carpet. Her face has still got that Italianate way to it and the eyes are as startling as ever. The blonde hair is even longer, falling round her shoulders.

I should talk to him, I tell her.

Maybe that's not wise.

I know he arranged my release, I say, and she brings her eyes up from the carpet and looks at me straight. Her eyelids flicker; there are lines beneath them but the eyes are as young as ever.

He didn't arrange it, she says. I did.

A wave comes up from the sea and hits the promenade, shaking the house. The pathetic fallacy, I think, and it's my turn to look at the carpet.

Tell me that again, I ask her.

He didn't arrange your release. I did.

Why?

She doesn't answer, but steps back slightly, which I take as an invitation and I walk inside. I try to stop my hands from shaking. Should I have guessed, I wonder, and does it matter anyway? But something tells me it matters a great deal. The smell of cleaning wax inside is like incense in a church. The old painting is still there, I am glad or indifferent to see, I don't know which. She is very close to me and her perfume overtakes the odour of wax.

Why did you do it?

I didn't want you to die.

Thank you. And he did?

No. He didn't either.

Can I see him then?

She looks at me, blocking my way. I lay one hand on her elbow to move her aside, and she puts her hand over it. There is an engagement ring on her finger, with a band of gold.

Are you sure you want to? she asks.

Yes, I'm sure, I say. I move her aside and she moves back in front of me and it's becoming like a waltz.

There's something I should tell you, she says.

Yes, I say, but I can't stand it any longer, whether it's her closeness or the hand on mine. I move past her. She follows me and then grabs my sleeve.

Donal—

That's my name, I say. I make it through the hallway and walk into his study.

But the study has changed. There's a bed where the green table used to be and beneath the mirror there's a dresser with a bowl and a jug of water. The typewriter is lying on the floor, covered in dust, and he's sitting by the window, staring out to sea. He has not turned; still the same old Gore pride as rigid as the grizzled mane of hair that's all I see of him.

Father, I say, and he still doesn't turn. I can feel her behind me at the door. As I walk forwards I see the sun gleaming over the silver lines of the chair he's sitting on and wonder why the chair is silver.

Father, I repeat, and I see the chair has wheels.

Father, I say for the third time, and then I reach him. He sits rigid in the wheelchair, turning neither right nor left. I touch his face and he still doesn't turn. The skin is cold and waxen as if he could be dead. But I can hear the slow rise and fall of breath. Death doesn't breathe, I think. His eyes stare out the window to the sea, his mouth moves slightly with his breathing and that is all. I look from him to her.

He had a stroke the week you left, she says.

Why didn't you tell me?

I couldn't reach you.

And how bad is he?

He can't move. He can't feed himself. He doesn't respond.

But I don't believe her. I whip the chair round to face me.

Talk to me, I say. The eyes look at me, then back to the window.

He sits there, staring at the sea.

Can he hear? I ask her.

I don't know.

How can you not know?

I tell you, I don't know.

I touch his face again. I feel his cheek. The eyes look at me again and away.

He doesn't know me?

He doesn't know me either.

She is crying. I walk over to her.

Jesus, Rose. I put my arms around her.   **87**

You loved him, then?

Didn't you?

I suppose I did.

Don't you now?

I suppose I do.

But suppose is not enough, I suppose, or presuppose, I don't know which. I should be livid with some emotion but I'm not. It's as if the real absence happened a long time ago.

And what do you do now, Rose? I ask.

I look after him, she says.

Can I walk him somewhere? I ask her, since I don't know what else to say.

If you keep him warm, she answers.

So we wrap him in his black astrakhan greatcoat and tie his Trinity scarf around his throat. We bump him gently down the steps and his body slopes forwards into her pressing hand with each bump. I wheel him past the railings towards the sea.

The wind has died down and the sun glints in the little scallops the water leaves. Occasional neighbours pass and some of them nod. Nothing has changed except him and yet he is stuck in a rigidity that implies no change. It is as if he has been like this for ever. And I think as I walk that it is strangely comforting to be with him and not have to listen. To have him beyond all argument. The wind rises a little and whips his scarf backwards so it strokes my face. And that is all the contact I need. We pass the stretch of sandbank where we'd stick the nightlines and some other kid is doing it now, stringing pieces of gut between two metal supports.

Do you remember when we'd do that? I ask him.

The wind ruffles his grey mane in reply.

The spade and the lugworms and the tide out, your trousers rolled round your ankles. No?

The wind parts his beard a little, in the centre.

Then back in the morning when the tide was out, we'd find the plaice or the codling or the dogfish flapping like sandpaper.

I enjoyed that, I tell him. I thought of it a lot when I was away.

His scarf strokes my face again.

Thought of you a lot, I tell him. I hope my going had nothing to do with it.

The wheels squeak in some kind of reply. Come on, Father, I think, where is that barely suppressed rage, those perfectly chiselled sentences, those austere denials of my right to be? His head lolls to one side and I push it upright with my hand. There are flecks of spittle round the edge of his mouth. I stop for a moment, feeling weak. His chair rolls on of its own accord and comes to a halt by a sagging piece of railing. I take in gulps of air and try to clear my eyes of the haze in front of them. His head has fallen sideways again against the rusting metal of the railings. Any fat has vanished from his face, the bones seem welded to the skin, he seems older and more impervious than granite. The eyes stare out to sea and flicker, regularly, to the right and left.

I'm sorry, I whisper. A priest passes by from behind me. The wind rises and whips his soutane and he glances at us both, as if expecting some obeisance. I let him pass, then walk forwards to the chair again.

I'm sorry, but I don't know what I did.

The eyes are following the boy now, who has finished

his line and is dragging the shovel back across the sand. I can't bear to wonder if they remember. I draw his chair away from the broken rail, turn both of our backs to the wind and head for home.

She was playing the piano when I came in. I wheeled him into the room and stood there in silence, the three of us listening to the music. She had improved since I left. He sat, with his head on the breast of his coat, looking towards the floor. I wondered was it music to him, or just sound, like the waves outside.

I should leave, I said when I heard the last chord.

Why? she said.

I couldn't bear it.

Don't, she said. Spend some time with him. Stay.

And so we ate together. She prepared the meat and I prepared the vegetables. How do you feed him? I asked her. With some difficulty, she said, and while we ate he sat there. She told me how she'd found him, on his back on the promenade like a beached whale. A passer-by had lifted him to the house, left him in her arms, where she'd collapsed beneath his weight. She'd visited him in hospital for weeks, sat waiting in a room for some sign of remission. The doctors had recommended a home, given his condition. But she couldn't countenance the thought of it and so moved him back home, and had stayed to take care of him.

So does that make you really his wife, Rose? I asked.

Don't be flippant, she said.

It was what he wanted.

Well, he didn't quite get there, did he? she said, and smiled.

She stood up, put on a blue smock and began to feed

90

him, looking truly like a housewife. I watched as she held his jaw down with one hand, fed him mashed vegetables with the other.

I can't watch this, I told her.

Why not? she said. It's the reality. You must have seen worse.

I thought of Antonio and the blood-spattered wall. Then I watched until I could stand it no more and walked outside.

I climbed the hill to Bloodybank and thought it odd that I'd only ever done this in search of Mouse. I reached the wooden door, third in a row of tiny cottages, and his aunt answered my knock. Her hair was the same bright blonde, a cigarette hung out of the same reddened lips, but the skin of her face had sagged downwards, grown bulbous. She answered me in slurred words about Mouse's whereabouts, told me he was in the seminary in Hatch Street pretending to take orders.

Why pretending? I asked her.

Might take them in, she said, but he won't take me.

She closed the door, drunkenly, and I continued up the hill towards the train.

The lights in Westland Row were so dim when the train pulled in, I almost fell on to the tracks. There was a black-out in force, I gathered, because of what they now termed the Emergency. I blundered through the streets, one hand against the sooty walls. I knew them so well, I realised, I hardly needed to see to find my way. Past the pillars of the church at Westland Row, the railings of Merrion Square, my left hand tracing the grey limestone of the Government Buildings. I reached Hatch Street and stood outside the collegiate house watching the black-garbed figures come and go. After what seemed an age I recognised the springy walk.

Mouse, I called.

He turned and squinted in the darkness. Then a broad grin filled the space above his ill-fitting collar.

In the name of Jaysus—

The obscenity fitted oddly with his costume and I suspected his aunt might have been right.

He bounded towards me, grabbed me by the elbow and propelled me down the street.

Quick, he said, before they spot me.

Who? I asked him.

They have their spies, he said. And I'm on their list . . .

He led me down two side-streets, through the back door of a pub.

Inside there was a line of wedge-like shoulders perched by the bar, a haze of cigarette smoke and conversation in low, barely audible murmurs. The barman squinted at Mouse's clerical garb, then obeyed his order for two pints. I sat down and felt the familiar warmth, the cloak of anonymity Dublin provides.

I think the vocation left the week you did, he said as the drinks arrived. He raised one in benediction. And I was sorry to hear about your father.

How easily it comes back, I thought. I drank the thick dark liquid slowly, remembering the sweet ease it brought. I thought of her, in the house with him. I wondered had I hurt him in more than the ordinary way.

Why do you stay on? I asked him.

Three squares and a cot, as the man said. Now tell me everything.

Where do you want to start? I asked him.

Start with how you got out.

A consular official in Barcelona, I said, one Jeremiah Noonan from Cork, provided me with a passport and transport aboard a coal-scuttle.

A coal-scuttle? he asked.

Ship, then. You know the thing.

A last-minute dash to freedom, before the walls came down.

Something like that.

Tell me everything, Mouse repeated. Everything. So I told him everything, everything but the drab facts. Stories of anarchists dancing with the bodies of disinterred nuns in a bacchanalian Barcelona. I have seen the future, I told him, and it worked for a week. An army without titles, which refused to march in step, tales of simple plain heroism, battles fought with handguns and pikes against massed artillery, the bombing of Guernica, the fall of Madrid, la Pasionaria at the barricades.

His incredulity grew as I lied. I adopted the plainest of manners, one that implied more horrors than it could ever recount. And I was drawing a crowd now. I scanned their faces, young, fat with Dublin indolence, and saw with some surprise that they were looking up to me.

Wounds, asked Mouse, any wounds? So I pulled up my shirt and showed them my appendix scar. A girl with a Claddagh ring fingered it in wonder. The bullet should have passed through, I told her, but lodged in the hip. Is it painful? she asked. As we speak, I told her, and downed some more whiskey and grimaced with the imagined pain. The girl snuggled closer to me as I talked, but I shook my head at her advances, intimating an injury that had left me less than a man. Someone else asked me to recount my experiences at a Republican gathering in the Gresham but I told him the prolonged effects of bombardment had made me agoraphobic.

Now tell me what was it really like, Mouse whispered as we staggered out after closing time.

So, I said, you saw through the hyperbole.

I've got the God's-eye view, he said, fingering his collar.

It was drab, I told him, drabber than you can ever imagine.

You're wrong, he told me, I can imagine drabness all too well.

Of course, I realised. You've got a prison of your own.

One that'll last longer than yours.

We had reached the barred windows of Hatch House.

They won't take pot-shots at you if you shimmy down a drainpipe.

My problem is in shimmying up.

He stared at a drainpipe that led to a window on the third floor.

You can leave, Mouse. Come home with me.

Where would I go?

Your aunt still speaks well of you.

Like fuck, he said.

He walked towards the pipe and tested it. Then began to climb.

Call me, he said, please.

I will, I said.

Why don't I believe you?

I don't know.

I do. Because my present state is too depressing. But tell me you'll call and I can imagine it's true.

I'll call, I shouted, then he put one finger to his lips and almost fell from the drainpipe.

Remember me to your father anyway. Then he slid open the window and was gone.

The train left me on the promenade with the moon illuminating the high swelling of the sea. I was light-headed. I had forgotten to ask about a key and found a handful of stones which I flung at the windows. Rapunzel, Rapunzel, I shouted drunkenly, let down your hair. She opened an upstairs window and her hair hung in the moonlight like a skein of rope. Did I wake him? I asked her. She shook her head and had half a smile on her face. A pity, I shouted, and she frowned so I shouted again. Don't you want him to wake? She closed the window and I watched the procession of lights down the floors as she made it to the hallway. Then the light showed through the amber glass on the door panels and the door opened.

She was wearing a virginal flannel nightgown, like a nurse's.

What's happened to you? I asked her. You've lost all your colour.

How? she said.

You brightened up this house once, now you dress like a nurse.

Because I am a nurse, she said, gesturing me to be quiet with one finger to her lips.

No, I answered, you're a wife.

A wife and a nurse, she whispered, letting me inside, closing the door behind her.

Besides, who's to hear?

No one, she said. More's the pity.

She looked at me across the width of my grandfather's picture and she shook her head.

You're drunk.

Not yet, I said, and walked into the kitchen. I reached up into the top cabinet where the whiskey was and found it empty. Doesn't he drink now? I asked her. You're being cruel, she said. I shook my head, not meaning to be cruel at all. I'm sad, I told her. I had so much to tell him. Tell me then, she said, pulling a bottle out from an entirely different drawer.

I wanted to tell him, I said, the things I enjoyed with him and why I could never tell him the things I enjoyed. I wanted to tell him how I wondered whether times of enjoyment that are never spoken of can be considered enjoyment at all. I wanted to tell him how in my Babylonian captivity—a phrase which incidentally he would have relished—that was the only question I could think about.

She poured two glasses on the table and sat down.

Now you tell me, I said to her, why that is.

She looked at me and drank. Her lip was seriously perfect over the glass.

What were the things you enjoyed? she asked.

Fishing, I said. But that was before your time.

You never tried to understand him, she said.

And you did? I asked her.

Yes, she said. I can honestly say I tried.

So tell me, then. The word tell in my alcoholic brain seemed worth repeating, endlessly repeating.

He was the kind of man that finds it difficult to tell things.

Don't say was, I told her.

All right, she said, and repeated. He is the kind of man who finds it difficult to tell.

To tell what, I asked her.

To tell of things of the heart, she said, and the phrase seemed to express a kind of loss in her.

So you noticed it too.

I was speaking with regard to you, she said. He found those matters difficult to express which created that difficulty in you which made it more difficult for him.

O rose, thou art sick! I quoted.

On the contrary, she said, I'm very well.

I was quoting, I said. It was a different rose.

I know, she said. The invisible worm.

I have no doubt, I told her, that it created that difficulty in me but what interests me is where the difficulty came from. I wasn't born with it, or wouldn't like to think I was. His difficulty was all his own.

If you like to think of it that way, she said. But remember you're drunk now and so you could be wrong.

Not yet, I said. Not yet drunk, I mean. I poured some more of the whiskey and expected her to tell me to stop. When she didn't, I reached one finger out to touch her lip.

So am I wrong? I asked.

Yes, she repeated, but let my finger stay on her lip.

So what did he tell you? I asked her.

Much the same as you're telling me, she said.

I don't believe you, I said, and I didn't. Her silence told me I was right.

The world turned wrong for him, she said. He wanted to make sure that didn't happen to you. He wanted you to be something. Then he was afraid you would reject what he wanted you to be.

So I did, I said.

Well, she said. That saddened him.

And did you love him? I asked, with my finger between the lip and the glass.

She drew her head back. My finger hung in the air, pointing at nothing in particular. She drank once, closed her lips, then opened them again. Her hair made two sheaves of wheat around her forehead. Her eyes were like the eyes of statues, pitiful and yet emotionless.

I did what you couldn't bring yourself to do, she said. I cared for him.

As much as you cared for me?

She stood up. She brushed her flannel nightdress with her hands.

There are things I won't let you say, she told me. You have to remember that, if you stay here.

You going to throw me out?

No, she said. But if you stay here, there are things you will not say.

What things? I asked her.

You know what things.

Perhaps I don't.

Then I will tell you when you say them, she said.

Do you promise? I asked her.

She turned to leave.

Rose, I called her.

She turned back.

If I promise not to say them will you promise—

What?

To tell me what those things are?

She left without answering. I finished the whiskey and listened to her feet pad through the house. I expected to hear the sound of the wheelchair, as she moved him towards the bed and lifted him inside. Then I wondered how she could have managed, with his weight, which could not have diminished that much. But there were only her footsteps crossing the floor, a piece of silence, then the soft creaking of the bed as she sank into it. So either he slept in the chair, or she had lifted him from it already. I sat there wondering did he dream, was his sleep any different from his waking. And were his dreams full of the words he couldn't say, full of the sounds he couldn't hear. I must have fallen asleep then because I saw his face bending over me, his mouth opening soundlessly in the attempt to speak. I tried to read his lips, but the beard obscured them.

I woke abruptly and saw the whiskey dripping from the table, the glass overturned. I got a cloth and swabbed the wet table and felt the absolute silence. I had a sudden longing for the bed of straw in that monastery cellar, the wheezing of Dai's damaged lungs and Antonio whispering from the corner about his imminent demise. I wondered should I have come back, should I stay here, should I have been born at all. It was alcoholic melancholia, I told myself, and I rose unsteadily and walked out into the hall. I saw their door was ajar. I walked gently forwards and pushed it open. There was a pale wash of orange from the streetlight angling through the room. He was lying by the window, a blanket tucked neatly around him, the silver of the wheelchair gleaming beneath him. So it spreads out into a bed, I thought. His hair was tufted by the pillow underneath his head, like filigree against the light. There was a chinois screen in the centre of the room. I stepped inside and could

99

see her beyond the screen, lying in the great oak bed. So that was it, I thought. I watched her for a while, the rise and fall of her chest under the blankets, until I got some sense and went to my room.

The next day brought sunlight, a great solid wedge of it coursing through the window. I got up late and could feel that tenderness round my temples, that moral unease brought on by too much whiskey. I made my way downstairs and wondered what I'd said last night. The kitchen was empty and the ochre walls were bright with the sunlight. I walked through the hall and heard the rustling of papers from the living-room. She was sitting by the window, thumbing through a pile of bills or letters. He sat across from her like a great immobile child, his head down and his mouth slightly open. She didn't look up when I came in so I decided to apologise.

I'm sorry, I said, if there's something I should be sorry about.

What kind of an apology is that?

None, I suppose. But I don't remember.

She lit a cigarette and looked up from her papers. The smoke did what smoke does to her face. Then she held out a letter.

Came for you in the post today, she said.

The stamp was from Spain. I saw the General's face again, with the three-cornered hat.

You've got friends over there? she asked.

I shook my head. I pulled back the envelope, which came away too easily, as if it had been opened already.

You must think me rude, she said. I never asked you

She dropped her papers and stood up.

Come into the kitchen, she said, have some breakfast and tell me.

We walked inside, leaving Father alone there.

Did someone open this? I asked her.

Jesus, Donal, give me more credit.

Maybe they censor the post?

You're in some kind of trouble?

I said nothing. I opened the letter and saw a scrawl of mathematical symbols. She cracked two eggs on to the range and asked me again about Spain. So I told her, the truth this time. About the journey to Madrid, the afternoon at the ambulance wheel and the incarceration. She laughed.

Don't laugh, I said to her.

I'm sorry, she answered, laughing more. But you must admit it's funny. After all that drama, the only action you get is an hour behind the wheel of an ambulance. Do you drive well?

I shook my head and began to laugh with her. No, I told her, it was truly heroic. I turned a corner and whacked into a fire hydrant. I could hear the gunfire.

You could hear it?

From about two miles away. Then a mortar bomb hit the house up ahead of me. I reversed back into a street full of loyalists.

Then prison?

She was smiling now, trying to hold in the giggles.

Safest place to be. Till you had to go and fuck it up.

I thought I saved you from a firing squad.

Actually you did, I told her. But only the sound of it.   **101**

How do you mean?

I shook my head. I thought of Antonio, probably two weeks dead now.

Leave it, Rose, I said. I looked at the letter again. I remembered Hans and his talk of the Heidelberg principle. Or was it Heisenberg?

She came towards me smiling, holding a plate.

Here, soldier, she said. Eat.

The hair was falling over her face. She sat down beside me, the smile a nostalgic, far-off one, watching me as I ate. The sun came through the window, lit one half of her face. It suddenly struck me that she seemed happy. She had in some indefinable way become a woman, since I went away.

What are you thinking of, Rose? I asked her.

I'm thinking you're going to have to pay your way.

With what?

Don't the war-wounded get pensions?

In this war, maybe. Not in that one.

Maybe I can employ you then, to take him for walks. A penny a mile.

No, I told her, I'll walk him for free.

As she settled a blanket round his shoulders I saw a tangle of wire glinting in the open cellar door. I walked down two steps and saw lying between the coal-scuttles two iron rods, the skeins of catgut and the row of fishhooks, a shovel beside them. I grabbed them all in a bundle and walked back up to where she had him perched in the open doorway. I'm taking him fishing, I told her. Fishing? she asked. Nightlines, I told her. Before your time.

The tide was out and the sun glinted as it had years ago, off the scallops of the rocks. I turned when I reached the promenade and saw her standing in the doorway, arms akimbo, watching us, her yellow hair bright in the sunlight.

She seems happy, I told him, as I wheeled him past the urinal, its great wings of concrete trying to imitate a pagoda. Did you do it, or was it me? Could it possibly have been you that opened her like a flower and let her breathe? That abstract, girlish air had been replaced by something different, something hard to define. If it was me, I told him I would leave, but if it was him I promised to stay. I could quietly delight in her happiness, his silence, as long as things stayed that way.

There was a ship out on the sea, unnaturally high on the surface of the horizon, some kind of battleship, metal grey against the hot sky. I've become a hero of sorts, Father, I said. A counterfeit hero. A hero of confusion or out of confusion. Should I go to public meetings and invent achievements, my suffering under duress, my prescience even, to have been a kind of harbinger to the Emergency we labour under? Will you not be proud?

But he wouldn't, I knew, or wouldn't have been. The sun must have been particularly hot, or the blanket round him, for there was a glimmer of sweat on his brow which gathered into a drop and trickled down his nose to his cheek. I could almost have mistaken it for a tear. Are you too warm, Father, is she too eager for your comfort and wraps you in blankets when your astrakhan will do? Or could it be a tear? I wiped his cheek with my hand and turned the wheelchair to face the battleship. Boats on the horizon had always meant a lot to him. Thoughts of the Americas, of the edge of the world, those days before Galileo when the earth was flat. Those monsters at the world's end, fabulous creatures whose pleasure was to whoop as the galleons tumbled through the void. Maybe he has chosen silence, I thought then. The battleship edged slowly past the crown of his waving hair. The world being so unspeakable, he would rather be mute. This condition was a blessing he would have desired.

I walked on again, and saw another tear gather. I thought paradoxically how pleasurable his silence was. Not because I wouldn't hear him speak, but because it was only his infirmity that allowed me to approach him without embarrassment, circumspection and all of those awkwardnesses that had made us what we were. Do you hear me, Father? I thought, and felt for a moment from his inert shoulders a resounding yes. But I leaned forward and looked at his eyes and saw them fixed upon the battleship, quite blue, with all the vacancy of cornflowers.

I pushed him on again to where the railings ended and the promenade moved easily and gently on to the sand. The sand was hard, strewn about with pebbles, and the wheels moved easily over it. When we made it to the point from where the tide had retreated, the wheels bumped and splashed over the ridged pools, his head jerked periodically. I apologised uselessly to him but pressed on. We reached the edge of the rippled water then and I faced him towards it, with his eyes fixed on the slowly moving fortress of grey. I took the spade then and dug, in the way he had taught me. I was rewarded with a handful of worms and jammed both rods on either side of his chair, the hooks swinging in front of his face. I skewered a worm on each hook, looking at his eyes each time for a hint of recognition. I felt the urge to talk, but kept it down, remembering the silence he used to maintain with me. When the work was finished and each worm struggled on its hook I stood for a while with my arms on his shoulders, looking out to sea. I remembered the wall of water in my dream and imagined the battleship carried by it, smashed against the shore like a child's toy. I felt the same peace again, the same lack of need for speech. I pushed him back then towards the promenade, wondering had he felt it too.

I spent the day in the house, with Rose and himself, seeing whatever rhythm they had established between them. She moved him from the front door to the back yard, following the movement of the sun. She worked through papers in his room, told me the details of his finances, which were almost non-existent. She played the piano in the afternoon. As the tide came in, the battleship passed out of view. I sat upstairs in what once was my room listening to the soft rustle of her Schubert. The music called for me to come down, play with her, share whatever mood it was we had before, but I didn't dare. I felt it was a chord between the three of us, threading through the house. I saw her cycling down for groceries at half past four, when the tide was on the wane. I went down and played myself then, the same tune she had played, as if to keep him company. When the light was beginning to fade, several hours later, I went to my room again and could see, way down the beach, my rods beginning to emerge from the retreating water. I went to Rose, who was in the kitchen, and asked her could I walk him once more. With a little luck, I told her, we might have caught something.

So I wheeled him down the promenade again, through the evening chill that was descending from the Head. He sat with the same rigid intensity and when I bumped him over the sand his spine hit the seat with the rhythm of a jackhammer. I could see a silver glint in the evening light, jerking between the rods. When we reached them I found seven mackerel hanging from the hooks.

We cooked them that evening, and the first pebble of our new existence fell into place. I had a function, however humble. I was a gatherer of flesh from the sea outside. I gutted them, Rose prepared them and Father sat by the radiator, his eyes on the metal bars, blinking regularly, as if aware of his impending meal. His breath quickened slightly as the fat began to spit. When he heard the chink of the bowl against the cutlery, I could swear I saw his lips move.

I wheeled him from the radiator to the table.

He knows something, I said to Rose.

Like what? she asked.

He knows food is coming.

You trying to be funny? She wiped her hands on her apron.

I could hear him breathing when the fish fried.

She opened his mouth and began to feed him gently, wiping his beard all the time, fork in one hand and cloth in the other. She ate herself while he chewed, then fed him again.

I never thought of fish, she said.

Why not? I asked.

The Emergency, she said. No meat to be had, so I cook potatoes.

Do you consider yourself his wife? I asked.

I've no one else, if that's what you mean.

That's not what I mean.

And what if I do? she asked.

Something in her tone made me bridle.

What did I do wrong, Rose? I asked.

Just about everything.

I touched her neck. She shifted away, slowly.

Tell me.

No.

Go on. Give me a hint.

I touched her again and she let my hand stay.

It's all connected, she said. Something broke in him when you left.

And is that my fault?

You could have stayed.

With both of you? You know I couldn't.

I would have gone, if you'd asked me.

The thing is, I said, you were his intended . . .

Perhaps I was. But that's connected too.

His plate was empty. She poured a mug of tea for him, put a straw in it and placed it in his mouth. The tea slowly vanished from the mug, silently.

I twirled one of her blonde curls round my finger.

Did you love him, then?

You must assume I did, she said.

She leaned her head back and eased the muscles of her neck against my hand.

But do you know what's more important? she said.

What is?

The fact that he may have loved you.

That's a very large assumption.

Call it what you want.

She got up, suddenly, dispelling my hand.

He'll sleep now.

How can you tell?

He has his habits, like any child. Help me.   **107**

I left her in his room, settling him in the dark, the sound of waves outside. I walked back into the kitchen and saw the letter, where I'd left it by the windowsill. I opened it again and looked over its incomprehensible hieroglyphics. I caught the word Scarlett. I knew that somewhere in the dark well of quantum physics, somewhere between the lines of *Gone with the Wind,* lay a code that would translate it. How appropriate, I thought, that he had written in a symbolic language that was indecipherable. Then I remembered his statement: that everything must be paid for. I felt a cold wind hit my spine and wondered what form my payment would take. I opened the grate of the range, placed the letter on the coals and watched it burn.

The next morning I took him for a walk again. It was fast becoming a ritual. I felt some expectancy in his shoulders as I pushed his wheelchair down the prom. There was a cold brisk spring wind and flecks of white on every wave-crest. The wind parted his beard in the middle, so he looked like a biblical patriarch.

So did you love her, Father? I asked him.

But of course, I answered. I could almost speak for him now. I could imagine his voice, like an apologia inside me. So we walked and talked of her. Rose, in all of her manifestations. Teacher, wife, lover, nurse. We decided we relished them all. I moved up from the prom on the path round the Head towards Greystones, bumping his chair over the rocky ground so his head jerked back and forwards as if in agreement with my musings. We can exist, I told him, in the illusion of perfect harmony. I passed the nest of a hedge-sparrow and leaned the chair sideways so he could see the sky-blue eggs. I pointed out a hawk to him, hovering at knee level by the cliff face. Nature seemed to complement our union. I told him about the Hitler–Stalin pact. He took this in with his familiar blankness, so I elaborated.

Don't you realise, I said, this means an end to all our arguments. Or to all argument. The beasts are in bed together. Or doesn't it make a difference? He stared at the metal plate of the sea below us and said nothing so I assumed it didn't.

I bumped him on to the smoother surface of the promenade. Figures passed us and nodded, elongated by the morning light. Then, approaching the house, I saw a burly shape leaning by the railings. In the shadow of the houses, a bicycle propped beside him. I walked closer and saw a policeman's uniform, topped by a thatch of cropped red hair.

Grand day that's in it, he said, in a thick Kerry accent.

Thank God, I said. I pushed the chair past him, towards the door. He followed, and spoke again.

You received a letter yesterday.

I stopped and nodded. I felt a familiar shiver.

So you would be Donal Gore?

Yes, I said.

Rose opened the door. She looked from him to me to Father. The policeman lowered his voice, conspiratorially.

When you're ready, sir, if you'd come with me.

I left Father with Rose at the doorway, avoiding her troubled gaze. You'll be back by teatime, said the policeman softly, touching my elbow with one arm, holding the bicycle with the other.

He walked me to the train and took a seat by the window, his bike perched incongruously beside him. Great weather these days, he said, despite the bother over the water. I asked him was I under arrest and he shook his head, smiled sagely and winked. A couple of questions, he said, that'll be the long and the short of it. When the train pulled into Tara Street he walked blithely with his bike from the carriage to the platform and out along the low wall by the Liffey. A grand wee country, he said, if they'd only leave us be. His cryptic statements seemed to demand agreement, so I agreed. The boys in the Castle, he said, have a great weight to bear.

The boys in the Castle turned out to be middle-aged with paunches, one with a small holster supporting his. We found them through a succession of low corridors, in a room without windows, lit by a gaslight. The guard who brought me stopped with his bicycle at the door, gestured me inside with a grimace of sympathy.

The thing is, one of the boys said, with no introduction, this will have to be investigated.

What will? I asked him.

The letter, said the second, the damned letter.

You will appreciate, said the first, we must keep an eye on things.

What things? I asked him.

Things from across the water, he said.

Absolutely, I agreed.

And your missive did cause quite a stir.

Am I to assume that it was opened?

Assume what you like, the second one said.

The thing is, the first one said, you'd never be up to the antics of that shower.

And what about the other shower? the second one asked. Sure they're even worse.

A silence fell as they contemplated the virtues of one shower or the other. I stood for a moment, then shuffled.

So what am I here for?

They both looked at me sharply, eyes bird-like, chins puffed beneath their collars.

To meet Mr Soames, the first one murmured. He nodded his head to his companion, who opened an inner door. There was a tallish gentleman sitting by the gas-jets of a fire, shoeless, the soles of his feet raised to the warmth.

Mr Gore, he said, and rose and stretched one hand over a sea of papers. Pardon us for bothering you. But you will appreciate the situation you find yourself in is rather delicate and could be interpreted in a number of ways.

I told him I fully appreciated that.

We could make two assumptions, he said. We could assume this letter came to you as part of some prior arrangement, in which case your complicity in an implicit act of espionage will result in your spending the remainder of the war—or should I say the Emergency—in the Curragh Camp. You know the Curragh?

I pictured the row of drab huts surrounded by sheep off the road to Kinnegad and assured him I did.

Or, he said, we could assume that this missive came of its own volition, without any complicity on your part, in which case you can spend the remainder of the war in any way you choose.

I told him the latter was the case, and to contact one Jeremiah Noonan at the consulate in Barcelona, a small officious Corkman with rigid sartorial standards.

We have already done that, he said. We found that your stepmother contacted Foreign Affairs in Stephen's Green with a plea to intervene on your behalf in any way they could. The resultant contact led to a member of the Abwehr conducting you from your incarceration near Madrid.

He took a long breath. The detective behind me exhaled.

You'd never be up to them, he whistled between his teeth.

I myself favour the second assumption, Soames continued. Which in turn leads to two separate courses of action. One can ignore this and any subsequent missives—for I have no doubt that more will follow. Or one can act upon it.

He let the silence in the room speak for itself. He looked at me, then away. The first detective scraped his shin with his fingers and did likewise.

First, I ventured, and found myself copying his syntax, one would have to divine what the missive contained.

We have made some progress, he said, and smiled softly. We consulted the professor of mathematics in Trinity College and found the key was Heisenberg's Leipzig paper on the uncertainty principle, published in 1927. Each equation is simply a reference to a page, a line and a word within that line. The only puzzle remaining is the colour code at the beginning.

Gone with the Wind, I said.

What? he asked.

Scarlett, I said. Scarlett O'Hara. And he calls himself Rhett.

And you, I am to presume, are Scarlett?

I nodded and found myself blushing.

He watched, enjoying my discomfiture. I broke the silence.

So what does it say?

It's a request for Scarlett to make all possible contacts with the Republican movement.

I looked at the floor. I felt the same chill again.

Why would I do that?

Why indeed? he asked. But you must now appreciate the extreme delicacy of your situation.

I told him I more than appreciated it. He leaned his face close to mine. Young, but older than his years, his cheeks round and owl-like, belying his stature.

What we want you to do, Mr Gore, he said, is nothing. Just keep us informed.

Informed about what? I asked him.

Anything. Any subsequent missives that come your way. Any approaches to you from the movement. Anything and everything.

You want me to inform, I said.

In a word. The alternative is the Curragh.

He smiled, and stepped neatly into his empty shoes.

Here, he said, is a copy of Heisenberg's Leipzig paper. If you need any help with the mathematics, I am at your service.

Could it be, I wondered on the train back, that the co-efficient of forces acting on any one moral choice would lead only towards betrayal? That the act of betrayal was now the moral one? I said the word to myself silently and lost myself in its resonances, its odour of bees, sand and lapping water. I would betray, having no alternative. But whom or what remained to be seen. I thought of Father staring at the radiator, and Rose smoking by the range, and realised there were depths to the act I had yet to plumb.

——

Over the next few weeks I laid nightlines religiously morning and evening, bought more so the promenade became festooned with a string of hooks. I waited for word of those I might inform on or inform, but none came. To pass the time, I began selling what I caught. I found shops in the city who were glad of anything that slipped by the ration books. We ate the rest, and soon with the money I made I placed a down-payment on a boat, nets, lobster-pots, lines. Meat and vegetables being scarce, I sold everything the ocean gave me. I laid lobster-pots from Bray to Dalkey, supplied every eating-house from Jammet's to the local chippers. I would read him the news of the war each morning, then row out with the first light to empty the pots, use the net and lines all afternoon. I would play with her in the evening, my fingers, which I could never quite free of fish scales, moving with hers over the keys. He would sit in the kitchen, quietly vacant, listening to the notes that drifted round him. We became a family of a kind, a warped reflection of one, but at least a family. Outside of time, of the ferocious time that waged round the continent beyond us. After a while I hired a local boy to help me with the boat. We extended our reach to beyond the Kish lighthouse, covered the coast from Wicklow Head to Donabate. And with the cash the sea now gave to me in fistfuls, I bought Rose a dress.

She had never added to her wardrobe since I left. She was eking out what was left of his pension, and the only new garment I'd seen her wear was the smock she welcomed me back in. She was brushing flour from it in clouds with her hands when I made the suggestion. I was feeding him from his plate his now familiar dinner of smoked mackerel. Rose, I said, with a new and heady sense of possessiveness, let me buy you something. You buy us enough, she said, with that slight air of tetchiness she used to disguise embarrassment. No, I told her, I want to buy you something. You, Rose. She looked at me and blushed. What? she asked me. Anything, I told her. Whatever you need to lift your spirits. My spirits, she said, don't need lifting. Does that mean you're happy then, Rose? I asked. Father had finished the plate. He stared at the fork absentmindedly. Maybe, she said, blushing again. All the more reason, I said. And why are you blushing, Rose? Am I? she asked, and blushed again.

I knew it had to be a dress, but let her lead to the suggestion. Any hint that her wardrobe was deficient would have driven her to silence, the kind of blush from which she wouldn't emerge for hours. So I fed him and listened, while she went from pots and pans to a music stand, a new coat for him, and eventually to what she so rarely allowed herself think of, herself.

We took the train, all three of us together. I lifted him from the platform with the help of two porters and sat him on the seaward side so the whole vista of the bay would be there for him. He shuddered when the whistle blew, and Rose gripped his hand as if to reassure him. I tried to share his perspective as the train drew off and the cold light over the Vico Bay drifted through the clouds of smoke. As to a child, it seemed, each new turn of the rails intimated a different world. Did he remember, I wondered, the countless times he must have taken this journey into the Government Buildings in Kildare Street? And if he didn't, what would he remember of now?

O'Connell Street, when we reached it, was like a drab spinster at a sister's wedding. The Pillar stretched up into the summer haze, the Guinness barges lolled on the Liffey and some essential life seemed to have departed from it all. We walked through the thin passers-by to Clery's clock, where a few sharp-suited youths waited for their women friends, dragging fast on cigarettes, checking their watches with the clock above them. Rose looked at the mannequin dresses and I pointed his wheelchair in the same direction. Their faces seemed to engage his, their eyes bright but unseeing, their mouths perpetually smiling.

Inside, the assistant presumed I was the husband. Rose, after her third dress, fell into that presumption too. She would emerge from the changing room and twirl for both of us, but her eyes went to mine. Each one she tried on brought a new glow to her cheeks, as if instead of putting clothes on she was taking them off. She chose eventually a whole outfit with cream and yellow stripes, as serene and buoyant as a deckchair on a hot afternoon. Then we walked together to the footwear department, and bought her a pair of laced high-heeled boots. A hat, I felt, would crown the afternoon. I wheeled Father towards a room replete with hats, each suspended at head height like a bird frozen in space, and she followed, all pretence at reluctance having vanished. The dress having freed her body, the shoes giving it height and poise, it was the hat alone that let her soar. Perched on her head, her hair bound up beneath it, it was blue, like a kingfisher, with a crescent of black lace at the front. I can't wear this, she whispered. Why are you whispering? I asked her, and she glanced from the assistant to Father, who was staring with intense concentration at a tailor's dummy. It seems, she said, profligate. Blame it on me, I said, and tilted the hat slightly and drew

her towards a mirror. She looked at herself, then away,

then at herself again. She stared, then smiled and became reconciled to whatever elegance it gave her.

We emerged on to a cooler O'Connell Street, with the sun going down. Fingers of red were beginning to colour the sky beyond the Pillar. We were drab once more, as drab as the street but laden down with parcels. On the train back Father looked at her with a kind of melancholy, or it could have been a trick of the light. Do you think he noticed? I asked her. Let's hope he didn't, she whispered, staring out the window at the blue swaths of Dun Laoghaire pier. Why do you say that? I asked, staring at the silver chrome of his wheels. I think you know, she said, with the kind of finality that made me realise I did.

She made dinner that night and lit candles, saying they were because of the blackout, as if to deny the hint of elegance they brought to the kitchen. I fiddled with the dials on the radio and found some dance music. You should wear your dress, Rose, I told her, as she served out the lobster I had caught the day before. No, she said, there'll be another time for that. The candles gave my father's face the gaunt look of a church statue. We ate in silence, listening to Glenn Miller, when the broadcast was interrupted and Lord Haw-Haw's voice drifted through the room, the precise and mocking Anglo-Irish tones drawing a flicker of life from my father's eyes. We stared at each other as the voice droned on about Churchill's imminent defeat, the bombs that would thicken the air over London, and felt quite removed from it all. Her eyes had acquired that glow again, the serene Italianate blue of Renaissance paintings. I knew what she had referred to in the train and could feel the clouds of its imminent arrival. I told her about Hans, about the letter I'd received and my meeting in the Castle. Every word, though, was an avoidance of the subject we couldn't broach. Will they intern you? she asked, and there was a sense of real fear in her voice. I doubt it, I told her, since they wouldn't have released me in the first place. So what do they want? she asked. To keep track of things, I told her, and described how the tall one had talked of the one crowd and then the other.

I wheeled Father to bed after dinner, opened out his chair and settled him in it. She came into the room behind me, and I knew that everything was changing. She took out the dress from its wrapping, held it up to her body and turned to gauge my approval. Goodnight, Donal, she said, her face tilted from the mirror as if waiting to be kissed. I knew if I'd acted on her implicit invitation, though, she would have denied its existence. So I left.

I lay awake for a long time. I heard the drone of an aircraft that must have lost its way, and wondered should I leave. As they were dependent on me now, leaving was out of the question, and I wondered did I create that dependence with this in mind. There were no unselfish acts, I knew that now, and my continued presence there could only accentuate that sense of a hot, cloud–filled summer's day before a thunderstorm. I must have fallen asleep then because I opened my eyes some hours later to the sound of tapping on the window-pane. Mouse was the first thought that came to mind and I blundered from the bed to the window as if I was back on the night of my mother's funeral. I pulled back the curtains, half expecting to see the short-trousered form there, the tousled black mat of hair over the pale face. But there was an adult there in a khaki greatcoat with a fistful of pebbles, throwing them upwards. I opened the window and caught the last pebble he threw. Gore, he said, Donal Gore. Yes, I answered, and knew the time for betrayal had come again. Be so kind, he said, as to come to the front.

He stood beyond the lip of the veranda as I opened the door, as if expecting to be let inside. Where can we talk? he asked as I closed the door behind me. Anywhere but here, I said. How about on the harbour wall?

Don't force me to be conspicuous, he said, but followed me anyway. How more conspicuous can you get, I asked, than throwing stones at a stranger's window at three in the morning? Two, he said. Ten past two.

There was a moon over the harbour, forcing itself through weak fingers of mist. His eyes scanned the empty promenade. You still feel conspicuous? I asked him, and led him down the seaweed-encrusted steps towards the boat. We stood then, on the gently shifting boards, and appraised each other.

You know what this is about? he asked after a silence.

A letter, I hazarded.

He nodded and took an envelope from his pocket. We couldn't make head nor tail of it first, he said. And who is we? I asked, more as a matter of formality than anything else. You damn well know who we are, he said. The movement, I suspect, I told him. Then, he said, we brought it to a mathematician in Trinity, who cracked it for us. Heidelberg. Heisenberg, I corrected him. The Leipzig paper on the uncertainty principle. Was never a great hand at the sums myself, he said. But you know this Rhett Butler? Rhett Butler, I told him, is a pseudonym. So I take it your

119

name isn't Scarlett? he said, and smiled for the first time. I know your name is Gore, he said. What I want to know is who's this other geezer.

A German, I told him, with intellectual pretensions. He interrogated me in a Spanish prison. Arranged my release.

So you two boyos had something in common?

You could say that.

He claims you're his only contact here.

He's wrong. I now share that distinction with you.

But you've met him in the flesh. Face to face.

Yes.

And he's the full shilling?

What do you mean?

I mean the real thing, the genuine article, not some two-faced fly-by-night trying to pull a fast one.

He wears the uniform of the Abwehr, I said, if that's what you mean. He made a pact with me. In exchange for my release, I would make certain contacts.

With us, he said. I nodded.

Then why didn't you?

The boat shifted under us. I looked at his face in the moonlight, eyes not at all unfriendly, mouth tough and uncompromising and a pair of shoulders bigger than an ox. The thought of him angry made me feel uneasy.

I thought, I said, if I bided my time one of you would come to me.

Wise, he said.

Because as we both know, I said, the walls have ears.

The times that are in it, he said.

What about them? I asked.

Turn your friend into your enemy.

And vice versa, I ventured.

But you're clean, he said. Above suspicion. You went with the commies to the bother in Spain.

On an impulse, I told him.

So where does your interest in the Hun come from?

England's difficulty, I told him, is Ireland's opportunity.

He stared at me hard, one hulking shoulder covering the moon. I held his stare, wondering would my story hold water.

Write back to him, he said. Tell him you've made contact with us. Tell him we'll come up with a shopping-list.

He turned abruptly and walked back up the barnacled steps.

Where do I reach you? I shouted after him.

You don't, he said. You'll see us when you see us.

I walked back to the house and felt unease in the air, like an evening mist. I took out the yellowing copy of the Heisenberg paper and scribbled on the flyleaf—Have made contact. Shopping-list will follow. I then thumbed through the pages of equations, descriptions of Jean's mirrored cube, of ideal coal-dust and ideal perceptors, and matched each letter of the note to a number. I wrote each number down on a virgin piece of my father's notepaper, stamped and addressed it and left it on the bureau. I woke to the same unease, walked down the promenade to post it. Then, with the envelope half inside the mouth of the letterbox, I changed my mind and pulled it back. They would intercept it, I knew, in the Castle, and I could save myself the bother and any further suspicion by handing it to them myself. So I walked over the tracks towards a waiting train.

Mr Soames, I requested of the guard in the hut in the cobbled yard. Tell him Scarlett wants to see him.

Your own name would do, Soames said, when I eventually reached him.

Aren't pseudonyms mandatory in these affairs? I asked.

What affairs are these? he asked.

Affairs of betrayal.

Who are you betraying? he asked.

Just about everyone, I said. And now that burly bogman who threw stones at my window last night.

Ah, he said with an air of someone reaching the inevitable. What was his name?

Wouldn't say. But he'd got hold of my letter.

How?

Through you?

He let me stew without an answer for a moment.

Said he was from the movement. So I wrote a reply and was about to post it to Germany, but thought I'd save you the trouble of intercepting it.

I handed him the letter. He let it sit there between us like an unspoken secret.

What does it say?

That I've made contact. That they'll be in touch with me later with a shopping-list.

You enjoy this, don't you? Soames said.

Not at all, I said. I thought I'd no option.

But you're good at it. The dead-pan delivery, the unconcern. You don't care, which allows you to enjoy it.

What I would enjoy most, I said, is to get out of here.

He smiled, and I stood. I moved across the room, then
hesitated.

Can't bear to leave? he asked.

The letter? I asked.

What about it?

Will you send it to them?

Why do you need to know? he asked, and I thought about it.

Thank you, I said. I don't.

On the train back I thought of whole stories of conspiracies and betrayals sitting on his desk, unknown to anyone but him. I wondered could I take comfort from that thought. As I trundled through the hills of eucalyptus bending towards the sea, I stared out the window and could see Rose, myself and Father as a triangular cocoon, an equation known only to ourselves that related to no known numerical system. There were energies there yet to be discovered, like the ones now blowing the world to shreds.

The weather itself seemed to match our triangular mood. Over the next week the sky stayed filled with a low cloud; there wasn't a hint of rain, but only the humid heat that brings the flies out. I worked my boats, tried to forget the business of betrayal, got to enjoy the muscular ease with which I could draw the nets. I stayed unwashed for the most part, left my body covered in a film of salt. The humidity kept the fish way down, so we began to journey farther out in search of them. From the Kish lighthouse to Howth, in a wide arc from Howth to Wicklow town, past tankers and coastguard ships and the distant specks of frigates on the horizon. The coast became a thin line behind us, our nets became entangled with porbeagle and basking shark, as if in the depths below us a more essential life was emerging. The swells were slow and strong, the sky seemed lower each day and yet the heat kept on, encasing us in its humid bubble. Then late one afternoon, four miles out from Baltray, the storm broke.

It was a southwesterly, whipping from the tip of Lambay Island, turning the sea into a garden of white. The boy yelled at me when I was dozing at the rudder in the heat and I turned to see the white froth around the island, the dark water advancing before it with the rainclouds over, as if being pummelled by unseen pellets. I kicked the engine into service and turned the rudder towards the mouth of the Boyne, where the pillars round the estuary sat still bathing in unnatural sunlight. It seemed impossible the one vista could be so peaceful, the other so full of fury, and I kicked the outboard motor into as much action as it would bear, the kid's hands bleeding trying to drag in the nets while his brother grabbed him by the waist to give him more traction. Then the wind hit us first, slewing us northwards; after it the rain and hail, like pebbles from above trying to pound us back into the element that held us, and after that the waves. Then the light was gone, and everything was water—the spray the waves threw round us, the rain driving from above; the shore vanished in a driving haze. There was exhilaration in the chaos, in the loss of all reference to boundaries of land, sea or air. I yelled at the kids to let the nets go, grab whatever they could while I hung on to the stern and managed to turn the boat straight into the breakers. The crash of each wave seemed strong enough to tear the boat asunder but I guided it straight into each crest, sensing any other course would pitch it over. I saw a guillemot whirl by upside down, a sheaf of lightning course through the hanging curtain of rain, then saw Lambay pass by me and realised the wind was changing. I was being driven out to sea and southwards. I thought of a grave in water: not a quiet meditative one, but the chaotic murderous wetness that surrounded me, and as a mountainous wave came towards me prepared myself for it. The one boy ran towards me and screamed, and then the other, the first with his hand held out and I grabbed, the other grabbed his and then the wave hit, as if the sea had been turned upside down to pummel us from below, then suck us in a long low wash towards itself but we, all three of us, managed to hang on. And after that wave had coursed down the gunwale and I saw both kids gasping at the stern, I knew, whatever it would throw at us, that we would survive.

Four hours later it abated; we found ourselves three miles east of the Kish, the motor silent. We pulled the oars out and rowed. The moon came through the scudding clouds and after a time even the clouds stopped moving. The wet and freshened air, an unnatural, clean severity about it all, not a breath moving, but the slow reluctant swells of the water as if it remembered what had gone before. The moon, percolated in the moving sea, and the sense of having survived, the godly certainty of it, the exhaustion behind every movement and the knowledge that after all that, one was still alive. There were fish leaping clear of the water but we couldn't be bothered to lower the nets. We rowed relentlessly towards Dublin Bay and thanked God we weren't a sailboat.

We found our way to the harbour and tied the boat to its cousin and I walked then, past the pub and boathouse to the terrace. There was a foot of water flooding the promenade. The lights in the house were on and she was standing at the door.

125

She had the kind of relief in her face that would have been unwarranted by anything but the flood, spreading down from the houses towards the Head, the moonlight reflected in it. She ran towards me, throwing up arcs of brine with her slippered feet, and fell on to my shoulders. Rose, I said, Rose, stop it, but I knew the words were no use, the gladness was unstoppable. It was as if I had arranged the chaos for her. I lifted her out of the water and waded through it myself, her chin embedded in my shoulder. She had lost one, she whispered, and couldn't bear losing the other. I told her to stop it again but knew I was lost in turn.

She brought me into the kitchen and stood me by the range; grabbed towel after towel out of the hot-press. I remembered her standing there all those years ago, Maisie drying her clothes off the range and wrapping my father's greatcoat around her. She wrapped the same coat round me now. Where is he? I asked her. She told me he had sat at the upstairs window all day, looking out on the storm. He always enjoyed storms, I told her, the play of lightning on the water. I bent my head to the towel she held out and let her dry my hair. Her fingers, strong like a peasant's, drew shivers from my scalp. I put my arms round her waist and undid the bow that tied her smock. The smock fell open and I traced my finger down her slip and felt the sharp bones of her hips and the suspenders beneath them. Donal, she said, Donal. I know, I said, what you are about to say. You don't, she said, and pressed her thighs against my hand. I drew her slip upwards and saw the garments beneath them, much like the ones she draped on the range when I was so much younger. There was the soft tinkling of the rigging of the boats out on the harbour. She kept kneading my hair until I raised my head and brought my lips to hers. She let me kiss her, her lips flat and surprised, her eyes wide open. I drew my hand up and traced the lines above her cheekbones. I've watched you grow older, I said. I drew her through the kitchen then, to the room where the piano was. I put the Rachmaninov on the gramophone and as the first chords filled the room stood looking with her at the water covering the grass outside, lapping up against the walls of the smaller houses, the moonlight tracing a broken line from above the Head. She drew me down to the couch then, opened my father's coat and put her arms around me.

We awoke with the first light. It was pale and aqueous, coming through the front window. I could see the calmed waters spreading down the length of the promenade. Rose's head was in my arms, her hair spreading over my chest like seaweed. I drew my arm from under her slowly and placed his coat over her dishevelled body. I went to the window. The water covered everything, the telegraph poles sprouting from it, the railings, occasional cars, everything suffused in its greenish glow. I thought of Father nearby and wondered had he felt her absence. I went into the kitchen, prepared some hot milk and took it to his room.

He was in his chair by the window, the blanket over his knees, staring in perplexed concentration at the vista outside. I stood by the door for a moment, waiting for him to turn. When he didn't, I walked towards him and held the cup to his lips.

Did you enjoy the storm? I asked him. The eyes turned towards me for a moment, the same perplexed, furious blue. They met mine, then turned to the window again. I brought the cup to his lips again and he drank, still looking outside. Did you miss her? I asked, to myself as much as him, and his eyes kept staring outside while he drank, obediently, like a child. I wondered what cognition went on behind those eyes, whether it was as innocent, as intuitive as that of the child he seemed to be. Then I wheeled him towards the door and along to the kitchen.

I cooked breakfast for the three of us. After a time Rose came in, everything neat now under her smock, her hair tied into a bun behind her head. Her eyes flashed to mine with a mixture of guilt and desire and I put a plate in front of her. Did he sleep? she asked me, and I told her that I could only assume he did. Her foot reached mine underneath the table and as I fed him strips of bacon I could almost imagine I saw in his face the hint of a smile. Look, Rose, I said, he's smiling. Bacon, she said. He always liked it.

Over the next few days the floods subsided, leaving a patina of brown sand over the promenade. I fixed my boats, bought some new nets and in between times wheeled him along the prom through the diminishing waters. He seemed inert and strangely peaceful, as if the lapping water everywhere brought a kind of quiet to him. I pushed him up the path to the Head and bumped him along the cliff walk to Greystones. I pointed out cormorants to him, a guillemot, a kestrel flying by with a mole in its claws. Do you remember, I asked him, you did the same for me? She was between us like a glue, it seemed, like the fringe of mist that sat on the horizon, merging the sea with the sky, merging the present and past into a continuous wave. I would return him to her in the house by the harbour, take the boats out when the tides were up and work the bay as long as there was light left. I would come back, stinking of fish, and find her at the piano, him sitting in the kitchen by the warmth of the range. The last traces of the storm had vanished from the promenade, but with it everything was changed. He was like a child between us, following our movements with his eyes, waiting on our ministrations, and we looked after him like one.

She became someone quite different. I noticed the odour of dried flowers, the feeling of an empty room in a country house on a hot summer's day. There was a field and we would wander through it, lie down on the places where the hayricks had been, mushrooms pushing up through the haystalks to fondle our backs. The traces of flour and baking powder on her fingers would bring me back to the country again, to a kitchen that opened out on to a cobbled yard where hens pecked and scrabbled at the handfuls of meal she threw them. She would lie on the sofa, the afternoon sun coming through the window, striking the dust we had risen from the cushions, and button the blouse again around her breast, Chopin playing on the gramophone, and she'd smile, as if she was thinking of something a long way away, and tell me the *Polonaise* was about to end. Then again, she'd say, draping her hair over the edge of the settee, you could always put it on again.

She was several people, I found. She was the Rose I had seen on the first day there, hair in a tumble as her stockings dried by the range, eyes smiling in an uncluttered, girlish way, promising friendship in her smile, and trying to be older than her years. Then she was the Rose I met on my first day back, the woman of someone's house, possessed by a destiny that emanated from upstairs, distracted, with the blonde hair uncombed and the eyes preoccupied. Then she was the Rose with the delicious and exact sense of her own pleasures, who would say no, wait, and clench her teeth as if the muscular rigour coursing through her could be prolonged for ever. A green light would come into her eyes, as if a forest had been illuminated inside her. On some afternoons she was the Rose her name implied, the roses you see on faded wallpaper and the patterns of dresses, an absolutely sweet presence in the odd arrangements of that household. On days when the light mist came down the headland and the sun broke through it intermittently, filling the rooms with a silver, elegiac light.

I could say I felt some guilt, but that would be a lie. One of those retrospective kinds of lies again. I felt no guilt whatsoever; each morning provided its own elation, I would rise, and walk to the shop by the station, buy the *Irish Times,* read what news there was of the conflagration over there. I would buy milk and bread and bacon and walk back as the sun illuminated the amusement arcades. She would be up by the time I came back, have the old man washed and cleaned so we would bump him into the kitchen again, I would comb his beard and hair while she cooked his—our—breakfast. He seemed sweet, like a child that completed our presence, the child we didn't have. His eyes with that cornflower blue that grew more startling every day, I would sometimes find them unaccountably on me, then when I turned away and back, would find them staring out of the window again. Birds would grab the attention of those eyes, the birds whose nests he used to catalogue along the walk to Greystones. I would read him the leaders from the *Times* as she fed him, and assume he understood. I could imagine him in any guise from his expression; the kindly patriarch, in the quiet autumn of his years, beyond all rage now, looked after by those who cared for him most. Or I could imagine a fierce intelligence behind those cornflower eyes, one that stared, saw everything behind their apparently random movement. Despair I could see there if I wanted to, hope that his condition would change, quiet devotion for Rose, the mother of all his attentions. I would imagine these things, maybe in lieu of the truth, which was, I suspected, that he took in very little.

Then one day I woke to find him sitting in his chair in the hallway, staring at a letter on the floor. I saw the stamp of the Reich and wondered had he somehow divined the full extent of my betrayals, before I realised his chair had moved. During the night, from the study through the open door into the hall. I wondered could he do in his sleep what he couldn't do waking, and imagined the thin hands pushing the wheels, motored by some dream. Then Rose came from his room, pushed him to the kitchen and I realised with a dull ache that none of us would be touched with the miraculous.

I opened the letter, fed him breakfast while I checked the scrawl of numbers against the Heisenberg. Scarlett, I could decipher. Rhett would welcome a shopping trip. Await your list.

I was emptying the wicker pots in Bullock harbour when I saw three figures dressed in greatcoats bumping on bicycles down the pier towards me. I saw the same broad shoulders on the first one and in the noonday sun his scale seemed diminished. Scarlett, he said, how's she cutting.

131

Donal's the name, I told him. Always Scarlett to me, he said. And while we're at it, meet Oliver. He gestured to the smallest of the three, who glared at me with protruding eyes through a pair of steel-rimmed glasses. No hand was extended, so I didn't extend mine. And this is Festy.

The third was long as the first was broad with hair half-heartedly slicked back, a greased lock of which dangled in front of his eyes.

And what'll I call you? I asked the broad one. Red, he said. A bit like yourself but with less of a stare.

You're a fisherman? asked the small one, Oliver, rubbing his left eye under the disc of his glasses with one finger.

For the time being, I said.

Would you grace us with a spin? he asked. Since the ocean, as far as I know, doesn't have ears.

I headed out for the Kish with the three of them and we bobbed in the wash of the Liverpool Ferry as it passed. You've heard from your friend, Red asked me, when the noise of the engine had died. Yes, I told him, he's planning a trip here. Even before he's got the shopping-list? he asked, as if there was an etiquette for such things. What exactly was on the shopping-list? I asked him. Funds, said Oliver, wiping the spray from his glasses. Funds for what? I asked. Silence came over all three of them for a moment, and they exchanged glances. Can we trust him? the tall one asked Red, and I heard the deep Cavan accent for the first time. Perhaps, said Red, we have no alternative.

Let me ask you a question, then, said Festy. If you were to strike at the heart of the enemy, where would you hit? I'd have to first find out which enemy, I said.

Would you stop your codding, you know the one I mean. England, the Crown, the whole damn caboodle.

Ah, old England is it? Well. I gave myself some time, and the appearance of what I hoped was reflection. The heart, I said, and ventured, Houses of Parliament?

He shook his head with a twinkle in his eyes. Think again, he said.

Buckingham Palace?

He grinned now, with obvious relish.

Again.

I give up, I said, knowing it would increase his glee, and it did.

Give up? Really?

Yes, I said, really.

Where, he asked, would you find the Royal Family, the War Cabinet, and the old dog Churchill himself all under the same roof?

Westminster Abbey on Poppy Day, I ventured.

Wrong again.

He lit a cigarette for dramatic effect, then finally came out with it. In a conspiratorial whisper, as if a passing herring-gull might have overheard.

Madame Tussaud's.

I drew breath, perhaps for the wrong reasons. He gripped my elbow, brought his lips closer to my ear.

Hit them where it hurts most. Their symbols.

Ah, I said. I tried to imagine his enemies melting into a ball of wax.

What a stroke, he said. George, Victoria, Anne, that old crone Elizabeth.

Milton, I said, Shakespeare . . .

Guy Fawkes, he said, with a certain lack of logic.

I nodded sagely and looked at the bobbing waters. I thought, thank God it's harmless.

We would need considerable funds, the tall one said.

Explosives, said the small one.

Weapons, said Red.

Must I describe the operation in detail? I asked.

What do you think yourself? asked Festy, his Cavan consonants thickening.

I thought even the Prussian Hans would have seen the humour in it. But I didn't say that.

Never show your hand is what I think, I said instead.

You think that's wiser?

Keep the cards close to the chest . . .

Maybe you're right. Or before we know it the Huns'll hit it themselves.

Better safe than sorry, I told him.

On the way back, while a porbeagle played around the bow, I told them Rhett had requested a meeting, and was awaiting details of the time and place. All four of us agreed to leave their operational plans in the realm of the unknown until that meeting had taken place. In cold print, I continued, the symbolic value of your plan would be obvious only to the most perceptive of minds. Better to explain it in person. The small one nodded, then the tall one nodded too and Red smiled. And there seemed more to his smile than met the eye. So what's the best place? I asked. Depends how he travels, said Red. By land, sea or air. By sea is the best, the submarine off the West Clare coast, Spanish Point strand, half a mile offshore on a good moonlit night. Put that to him, and tell him we've got just the vessel to pick him up. Which vessel is that? I asked. The one we're standing in, he said. And the tide was up, so he swung himself in one leap on to the granite surface off Bullock pier, now level with the boat.

We'll be in touch, he said, rolling his trouser-leg inside his woollen sock. Then all three of them mounted and cycled off into the grey afternoon.

Spanish Point, said Soames three days later, staring at the rain that spattered on the cobbled courtyard outside. I used to summer there, in the Eagle Guesthouse, nuns walking on the windswept beach below.

What have nuns got to do with it? I asked.

They have a summer home there. Spanish Point, he said again, as if the name awoke sentimental echoes for him. I suppose it has historic resonances.

The Armada? I asked.

The sea was red, they say, with the blood of Spanish sailors. He twirled my coded letter in his fingers.

Madame Tussaud's, he mused. They can't be serious.

Maybe they're not, I said. Maybe they have quite different intentions.

Or maybe, he said, they see some symbolic virtue in it. Explosives, landed at Spanish Point. Used to blow up the waxen image of Sir Francis Drake.

So what will you do? I asked him.

Send it, he said. And symbolic or not, when they move we'll move.

But before either moved, my father did.

III

The day he moved again there were low clouds hanging on the skyline like a membrane, ready to burst. To believe the weather affected our moods would have been fallacious, but I remember each moment with the skies that accompanied it, so the presence of rain, the heat in the house, the winds moving the rigging in the harbour behind us all come to have a spurious significance. A relationship, like a chord that accompanies each note of whatever melody we made, so the skies on this day stick with me, the grey-blue sack hanging over the sea, the occasional curtains of soft rain moving towards us. I woke early and checked them through the front window as usual. I left Rose sleeping and went in to check him, sleeping on the bed I had made of his chair, the woollen rug tucked around his chin. I put one hand on his and when his eyes opened, raised him gently to a sitting position, then moved him

136

slowly out into the hallway. I set him by the window in the kitchen, with the view of rough sky beyond the chimneys he seemed to like so much, and laid out the things for his breakfast. I let the eggs brown around the edges and the strips of bacon crinkle the way he favoured them, made the tea, then wheeled him to the table. And I was bringing the fork towards his mouth when I heard the sound of nails scraping off a wooden surface and realised his hand was moving.

It was moving towards the sugar-bowl, like a stiff crab, the veins standing out against the mottled skin. I looked at his eyes and saw them staring back at me with that sad intensity, his mouth pursed with the effort. I held my breath and watched the hand cross the acres of board to reach the bowl and grip it. I tried to speak, tried to encourage him but no sound came out. Then I saw the hand shake with a heroic inner fury and the bowl was overturned, the sugar spread in a neat arc beneath it. The eyes seemed to well up with tears then. Don't worry, Father, I managed to say, you tried, and reached out a hand to his face, but he almost imperceptibly jerked it away. I could see the mouth then pursing with a further effort and followed the line of it, down his twitching shoulder to his wrist to his hand, gripped crab-like as before but now with one finger extended, tracing a line in the spilt sugar. One unsteady stroke downwards, then two more to reach the centre of the first. It was a K, traced with all the awkwardness of a child at kindergarten. Then another downwards stroke and another with a stroke to meet it at the base. I L. He then repeated the L, began to form another letter but I already knew what it would say. Kill me.

His arm fell to his side, as if exhausted by the effort. It

touched the sugar-bowl as it fell, sent it spinning like a top, the sound of its rocking gradually diminishing into silence. And when the silence came it was absolute. His hand hung by the chrome wheel, his shoulders slumped forwards, his head bent at an odd angle, eyes staring sideways at the message he had written. Do you mean it? I asked him, but there was not a whisper of movement in reply, as if he had said all he could, or would. Then it was my turn to cry. The tears came quite independent of me; they streamed down my face unbidden and splashed on to his inert hand. Odd, since I was feeling nothing. I knew what I should feel: grief, guilt, an unutterable sadness at the thought that he could see, feel, perceive from his solitary cage. I thought of these things, should have felt them, thought I should have felt them, but the only hint of feeling was in the film of salt water that covered my cheeks. I am sorry, I said to him, I should have realised, should have felt more but can't. Please tell me why that is? He stayed slumped there, his breath gradually quietening, as distant and unapproachable as he was when I was ten. I heard the sound of Rose's feet coming down the stairs and ran my hand over the mess of sugar on the table, obscuring the letters.

She came in and touched her hand to my cheek and felt the wetness. Who made the mess? she asked. He did, I told her. How? she asked, and she must have sensed something for her hand went to my other cheek and began to wipe it. He moved, I told her. He moved? she said. He can't move. Well he did, I said. She put her hands round my shoulders. Don't, I told her. Why not, darling? she asked. Because he moved, I told her, he moved and he knows. My God, she said. Yes, I said, my God. He sees things. He hears things. He feels things. Don't you, Father?

He sat beneath us, head still inclined at the same angle, eyes staring at the spot on the table where the letters had been. I don't believe you, she said. You don't? I asked her, and I stood and grabbed her hair and kissed her. Her lips struggled against mine and I saw his head give a tiny jerk away from us to avert his eyes. Did you see that? I asked her. No, she said, and I grabbed her again and brought her mouth forcibly to mine and twisted her round so she could face him, see the head jerk once more, a small spasm run through his body this time. You saw that? I asked her. Stop it, Donal, she said, and now she was crying. I'll stop, I told her. But you saw it. Yes, she said, and now it was her turn to cry. Doesn't bear thinking of, does it, I said, to no one in particular this time. No, she agreed. It doesn't. What do we do? What do we ever do? I asked her. Take him for a walk.

I wheeled him out into the same low clouds, the rain still holding off but a fine mist blowing down from the Head. The mist, deceptive in its wetness, soon brought a fine dew to his beard. So you hear me, I said to him, you've heard everything I've told you. The back of his head kept the same rigid aspect towards me, moving only with the movement of the wheels. And you know, you old goat, you know everything probably and if you don't know you can guess. And I can only apologise. I'm sorry that it happened in precisely that way, that it happened when it did, between us and you, but the one thing I can't be sorry for is that it happened at all. Do you get my drift, Father? The wheels swished along the wet cement in reply. The dew glistened from his grey hair and that was all. I walked him past the empty gazebos, waiting for some sign from him, but got nothing. We came to the end of the railings, where the sand bled on to the cement of the prom, and I turned his chair left and pushed him towards the sea. I halted just at the lapping tide and left him facing the water, sat down on the wet sand and looked at his profile. It was rigid, like an immobile hawk, the blue eyes fixed on the horizon. Come on, Father, I said, and at the word father, the eyes flickered towards me. Father, I said, and the eyes flickered again. Look at me, I said, and the head turned slowly to face me, the eyes fixing on mine. The fury seemed gone from them, the wide, staring fixation, they were moist and melancholic like the mist all around us. Can you hear me? I said, Donal, your only son. I've done you wrong, I said, and the eyelids blinked, rapidly. Does that mean yes? I asked, and they blinked again. Or was it a no? I said, and they continued blinking. This is frustrating, I told him, I'll have to choose silence like you. The eyes blinked once more and I gave up talking. I sat there, laid my head against his inert arm and looked out on the sea.

And the silence brought a kind of peace. I could feel the occasional twitch of his arm and felt glad he was alive. I saw the line of the horizon gradually merge with the cloud and saw the rain coming towards us. I sat until the last possible moment, savouring the illusion of a union, then walked him back along the promenade as the rain sheeted down. We were both wet through when we reached the house.

I couldn't speak to Rose. I left him with her in the hallway and called up the boy and together we readied the boats in the driving rain. We chugged out beyond the Kish and let the nets out and drifted. The line of the bay was like a soft brushstroke, barely visible through the falling water. I could have cut the nets and drifted for days, left them both to themselves, to whatever silences would persist now between them. I could have drifted to Belfast, Liverpool, to the Isle of Skye, to some Norwegian outcrop where the language would have given me a different kind of silence. The thought of it was beguiling, seductive even: to leave behind whatever shards of life were left, to let that small smudge that was the Irish coastline vanish gradually into the mist that almost hid it. I was about to do it when I was brought back by a shoal of mackerel.

The pattern that the spitting rain made on the water's surface was thickened suddenly and I thought the showers had strengthened. But they hadn't; it was an explosion of sprats peppering the water all around us and after them the silver-blue flashes of the mackerel, foaming when they hit the nets like froth on a horse's mouth. The net was full in what seemed an instant; we pulled it in, dumped the slapping silver on the bottom of the boat and dipped it again. It filled as quickly and we pulled and dipped again till the weight brought the water almost to the gunwale. Then we headed for home.

So I was brought back to him by fish, once more. The rains had stopped when we made it to the harbour and got to shovelling the tons of gasping silver that weighed down the boats. We worked till midnight, packing them in ice, became covered in a sheen of silver scales ourselves and when the moon came out, we gleamed in its light. I made it to the house then, left the boy to arrange to get the catch to Dublin. She was sitting in the kitchen downstairs, the whiskey bottle open beside her, a cigarette smoking from a saucer on the table. She told me I stank of fish.

I know, I said, and poured a glass for myself. What did he do all day? I asked her.

The same as usual, she said.

But he knows.

How do you know he knows? she asked me.

So I showed her. I overturned the sugar-bowl and spelt the words he had spelt in the granules.

She stared at them for a while, saying nothing. So what do we do? she asked.

What do you mean, Rose? I asked her softly.

You're his son. For once in your life you could obey him.

You're serious?

No. Not serious. Jaded. Exhausted. I never thought things could be like this.

You wanted them so, Rose.

No. I wanted you. It happened.

I thought I could leave today and never come back. But I couldn't.

I know you can't. Neither can I.

She reached her hand over to mine.

I think I'm going mad, she said, in a quiet, matter-of-fact manner that made me believe she was. I spent all day with him, talking. I told him everything twenty times over. I was hoping for something from him. Some response. But nothing came.

She smoked and drank a little.

He's a vegetable, Donal.

He spoke to me.

Then he's playing a vegetable.

You hate him, do you?

Sometimes.

I could say nothing more to her. I put the wireless on and we listened to talk of the war. I fiddled with the dials and found some music, a marching tune with heavy brass, made distant by the interference. I walked behind her then and put my arms around her. She held them to her breast with one of her hands and reached the other back to grip my neck. The fish scales gleamed on my arms. Do I still stink? I asked her. Yes, she said, and drew me down on her knee and kissed me like a man. I knew then she was stronger than both of us.

I slept in his room that night. In the hope of discovering some secret life he lived while the house slept, of dreaming a dream he dreamt, of hearing him talk in his sleep, I wasn't sure. He lay still in the moonlight, breathing softly, staring at the ceiling. His breath rose and fell with the rhythm of the waves outside. They moved in counterpoint with each other, meeting intermittently, then departing again. In my sleep I was walking with him again, both of us barefoot over the wet sand. I looked behind me to the nightlines, far away by the thin line of tide, etched against it like dark spindles. We were making our long way back to the prom-enade; not a word passed between us, just the old silence, the comfortable one, the one that didn't ask for speech. I could see a dim plump figure on the promenade, wearing an apron, rubbing her hands in it with a distracted air. I could hear a low rumble behind us. I turned and saw where the nightlines had been a white line of water. The rumble grew louder. There was a man now, running on the promenade towards the house, a figure in black, a black bag swinging neatly in his hand. Father gave a strange strangled cry, like the squawk of a herring-gull, and began running too and I tried to follow him but slipped and heard the rumble grow into a roar, and then the white wave was on me, on us both, dragging metal rods and lines and hooks

143

in its wake. I saw through the whorls of water his face cry out silently as he went down.

And the next day it came. Falling through the letterbox on to the linoleum, its plain white envelope and Swiss stamp too prosaic for the contents inside.

Tuesday, the twentieth, murmured Soames, tapping the scrawled symbols with a manicured nail.

Why Tuesday? I asked him.

A full moon and a high tide. The beach drops thirty fathoms two hundred yards out. They'll get as close as they can, of course.

And you?

We'll be there, don't worry.

I looked across the square. Two G-men leaned on a battered Ford, eyeing me back.

You'll all be there. So I can take it that I'm finished.

Hold your horses. You've still to inform your Republican friends.

Ah. And when I've done that, I can stop this charade?

You sound as if you're not enjoying it.

I'm not. And my father is ill besides.

There must have been a hint of self-pity in my voice, for he looked at me directly and I could only think he'd never done that before.

Call me when you've spoken with them and we can forget these meetings ever happened, if you like.

I would like that very much.

Really? he said, with a note of disappointment.

I'm sorry, I said, and wondered why I was apologising.

I thought we could have moved on to Heisenberg.

144   Read the paper, rather than appropriate the symbols.

In other circumstances, maybe. I stood there awkwardly, wondering should I shake his hand.

A drink some evening, he said, when all this is over. And he held out his hand and I shook it.

When I stepped off the train at Bray I could see them on the promenade, three figures, each in a version of the same coat, trouser-ends bound by clips, wheeling bicycles. I gained on them rapidly, silently and allowed myself to enjoy for a moment the pleasure of observing them, unobserved. An early moon hung low over the low tide and it seemed a perfect evening to put this all to rest.

Gentlemen, I said, and the short fellow—Oliver, was it?—dropped his bike while the taller one performed a balletic whirl and in no time at all had me pinned against the railings.

Got a joker here, have we, he said, a comedian, while those strong bogman's fingers kept a relentless pressure on my neck.

I was happy, that's all, I said, prising his fingers away.

Why so fucking happy? he asked.

Because this little drama might be over.

When will it be over?

On the twentieth. Spanish Point. He's coming.

You know this character?

I have a passing acquaintance.

You'd recognise him?

I nodded slowly, realising it was far from over.

We'll want you there, he muttered.

I looked from him to Red, wondering why.

What good would my presence do? I asked, knowing the answer already.

145

We need him identified, Red said.

Been sold a pig in a poke before, muttered Oliver, who had recovered from his fright.

Check into the Spa Hotel, Lisdoonvarna, the tall one said. Three days before. Wait there for word.

Why Lisdoonvarna? I asked. Why not Spanish Point?

Only draw attention to yourself. You've got a wife, haven't you?

And an invalid father.

Perfect. You're taking the waters, if anyone asks.

What waters?

The spa waters, you numbskull. The sulphur waters. The cure. For gout, arthritis, ringworm. Any ailment you can think of.

I watched them leave, three brown figures on wheels, their cigarette smoke curling behind them in the evening air. I paced back and forwards on the promenade and realised I was knee-deep in it now. Lisdoonvarna, the Spa Hotel, the sulphur springs—I wondered how I could explain this all to Rose. I looked at the moon, higher now over the rising waters, the scalloped sand being lost under a wash of silver. I imagined those sulphur springs like that tide, creeping slowly over his inert body, and thought why not try it, who knows, it might do him some good. Then I felt ashamed at the thought, justifying this honeycomb of betrayals I'd made through some half-baked hope for him. The tide crept in farther as I walked back, the kind of movement you imagine you see, and the water seemed to whisper the tale of its curative powers. But this is sea water, I thought, brine that cures nothing.

I went inside to Rose and saw her wheeling him through the hallway to the kitchen.

Do you think a change might do him good? I asked her, again surprised at how easily the deception came.

How do you mean?

He stared at the moon through the kitchen window.

We could take him on a trip. To Lisdoonvarna.

Have you ever been there? She was smiling now.

No. I heard of the Spa Hotel, the sulphur waters. Something about a cure.

You don't believe in that. You of all people.

Rose, I'm desperate. Or we are. Aren't we?

My father met my mother there. She smiled, abstractedly. They have a matchmaking festival. In September, though.

We need a miracle, don't we? I said. I was beginning to believe it myself.

I left her to think about it, with that smile on her face, the imagined memories of her parents' romance, and walked him towards the station. Would a miracle help? I asked him, as we walked past the bowling green. It was sodden as usual. I stood him under the awning so he could watch whatever trains arrived and went to the telephone kiosk to make my call. I pushed button B when I heard the G-man's voice and asked him to get me Soames. Wait a sec now, he said with that harassed voice of his, and I heard a door open and another figure enter and imagined the drab green room, the filing cabinets with the weapons belts hung up inside them. Then the telephone was lifted and I heard Soames's rather feminine tones. I told him what they'd asked me and heard his intake of breath and wondered would he have been lonely without me.

Donal, he said, it is essential you keep this appointment. **147**

I never miss appointments, I said. But for this one I'll need transport.

Take the train to Gort, he said, and the bus to Lisdoon-varna. Each name he mispronounced, in that half-English way of his.

No, I said, I have an invalid in my care.

An invalid?

My father. But don't worry. He'll provide excellent cover. We'll dip him in the sulphur springs and pretend to pray for miracles. But I'll need a car.

I heard the intake of breath again and imagined the silent swear, could almost see the pencil jotting down the profit and loss on the notepad.

Meet me tomorrow.

And a full tank of petrol—

Yes, yes—

And expenses for the three of us.

Three?

Rose, my, ah, stepmother.

Meet me tomorrow—

I went to put the phone down.

But Donal—

He was getting altogether too familiar, I thought.

Not here.

Where?

By the gasometer in Ringsend. This is serious expendi-ture.

These are hardly frivolous times. .

Rose, when I came back, had more than thought about it. She was positively ecstatic. She told me of trips to Mill-town Malbay when she was a child, her memories of the

Cliffs of Moher, of the explosion of white on the white-thorn bushes round the Burren. We've been living in a glasshouse, she said, it will do us good to be away. And who knows, she added, maybe. Maybe what? I asked her. She described a holy well she remembered near Moher, with a row of crutches outside. Someone must have brought them. So someone must have left them. Who knows, maybe something might happen. And what, I asked her, would we do if it did?

We were damned, I knew that, taking the train into Dublin. If he got better we were damned, if he got worse we were doubly damned. Deceit, I realised, had become my element. Betrayal, a kind of destiny. The choices led to nothing but betrayal, and any way out was by way of betrayal. By Sandymount Strand, a row of cormorants raised their wings to the air, like phoenixes. But her excitement, now that I had awakened it, was infectious. The thought that something might happen, anything other than the paralysis that surrounded us. The steam cleared from the platform at Westland Row, exposing a line of newspaper-sellers. I registered dimly some news about the Eastern front. I made my way out to the street, walked down past the church and turned right on Pearse Street, towards Irishtown. I turned left again by the Grand Canal and walked towards the dull silver citadel of the gasometer. As the river came into view behind it, I saw a figure standing there and recognised Soames's brown crombie.

There was a black Ford Prefect behind him.

Do you realise, he said, the lengths I had to go to get this?

I apologised and told him that with my domestic situation public transport was out of the question.

Not only the car, he muttered, but the petrol, what with the shortages and the like.

I told him not to worry, asked him what better cover could there be than an invalid father in a wheelchair. He sighed, nodded and handed me the keys.

And not forgetting the cash, I said, for board, meals and the occasional libation. He looked over the brown waters of the Liffey and took a roll of notes from his pocket.

The Chief, he told me, is most concerned that no untoward incidents occur.

Which Chief would that be? I asked.

De Valera. Neutrality is as you know his Bible and in a sense, the only begetter of all these events.

So it has reached his ears, I mused.

He handed the roll of notes to me. I thanked him, and watched him head towards the river, making a forlorn figure against the giant spiders of the dockland cranes.

When I got home Rose was packing cases and she told me my father had been smiling all day. How do you mean, smiling? I asked her. I mean, she said, that slight upturn of the lips which indicates pleasure. Pleasure at what? I asked her. At the anticipation of a trip, she said, a holiday, a breath of fresh air. The thought of a journey, she said, brings its own anticipation, often more pleasurable than the journey itself. So we should thank our lucky stars. And at dinner that night, over the last of our candles, the rippling shadows did seem to bring a hint of a smile to his face. He sat absolutely still, the fringes of the beard at his lips curling upwards. There seemed to be wisdom in his stillness, a sense of peace, rather than the customary rigid, furious torpor. Could it be that you are happy, Father? I asked him rhetorically, as I cleaned up the dishes. I could hear the sound of Rose's piano coming from the inside room. She hit a chord that sounded like a resounding yes. You must remember Lisdoonvarna, I told him, you would have passed through it during the Clare Election in 1917. There is a spa there, sulphur waters which make the blind see and the lame walk. Or at the very least provide some relief from arthritis. And maybe, just maybe, you might be blessed with movement or speech.

His eyes looked to my left-hand shoulder, their vivid blue undiminished by the candlelight. If anything they seemed more piercing, with a calm and untroubled insight into all my subterfuges, so I left him, and walked into the living-room.

Rose was playing some Lully. I put my hands on her shoulders and began to massage her back. The notes faltered slightly.

Do you feel, she asked me, the sense of things about to happen?

Yes, I said to her, but the question is what things.

The time when all the notes fall into their place, easily, without apparent effort. Remember how I taught you to will the music out so your hands obey the patterns underneath it?

I remembered, and my hands on the back of her neck told her that.

Just let's hope, she said, he keeps smiling.

It could be only in your imagination, Rose.

If it's in mine, she said, it's in yours too.

When I opened out his chair that night his lips had the same mellowness. Pleasant dreams, I said to him as he had said to me when I was a child. She was still playing downstairs when I laid my head on the pillow in my room. I could hear the slight pause when she turned each page of manuscript, and then silence. I heard her footsteps up the stairs and then crossing the landing to my door. I turned and saw her unwinding the long skein of hair, which seemed red in the dim light. That was the last of the candles, she said, so we must be going.

We are going, Rose, I said.

You don't know the relief in the thought, she said. And when I saw him smile it made me feel better about it. It's my fault, isn't it, she said, coming towards me.

What, Rose, is your fault?

I needed this house, she said. When I came here first I knew I needed it and it needed me in a way. He asked me to marry him and it had given me so much I had no option but to say yes. Then when you left I realised I had said yes to the wrong thing.

As long as you didn't say no, I said.

I took the hand that was hanging over me and drew her down to the bed. I traced my fingers down the freckles below her neckbone and she arched her head back, straining with the pleasure.

The thought that he might get better makes it easier, but if he did get better it might be worse again. So I'll be happy with the thought, she said. What do you think?

I told her that every move I made was a betrayal of something, and that even the attempt to end the betrayal was a betrayal again.

That sounds like hell, she said.

Maybe it is, I said.

So are we in hell then? she asked me, and crawled in beside me, her body so warm it almost hurt.

We are taking a trip, I told her, going on a journey. That's all. And that seemed to calm her. I felt her arms around my waist, heard her breathing soften, and she told me once more of the road with the snowdrops on either side, stretching through the low stone landscapes and the well with the row of crutches outside it.

The next morning I got up early and pulled the back seat out of the Ford Prefect and measured what space there was inside. I went back into the house and while he still slept, measured the distance between the wheels of his chair. I carried him out then, gingerly, so as not to wake him, and levered his chair into the space where the back seat had been. And he fitted, to my pleasure and surprise. To his surprise too, I realised when I walked round the other side and saw his eyes slowly wakening, his breath steaming the glass of the car window. I rolled down the window and waved to him. The eyes stared out at the promenade behind me. I wondered did he remember the black limousine that collected him each day when he worked for the Free State government.

We're going for a drive, Father, I said. A trial run, to test this new arrangement. I got into the front seat, turned the key and as the engine coughed to life, watched the slight vibrations that shook his body. I drove slowly, out the promenade road, watching through the rearview mirror his reaction as I hit each pothole. He seemed untroubled, staring at the row of seafront houses that went past. I stopped at the railway cottages beneath the Head and told the boy to mind the boats for the next week or so, peeled some notes from the roll Soames had given me, to tide him over. I drove back then, with Father's gaze now firmly set

153

to the sea. The landscape I had walked him down so often went flashing by with twice the speed. When I reached the house, he was staring out through the open window at the Head, with that secret hint of a smile on his face once more.

Rose had her flower-patterned dress on and was packing a hamper. He enjoys it, I told her. What? she asked. Motorised transport, I said. It makes him smile. She smiled too, and followed me to the door when I carried out the cases. She stood there, flowers all over, hamper in one hand, looking at him, rigid in his seat within a seat in the back of the Ford, and a gust of wind lifted her dress, making a taut umbrella round her legs. She laughed, didn't seem to care and pulled the door closed behind her. She walked forwards and the wind gusted again, weaving her dress round the hamper. Don't look, she said. Can't help it, I told her. Neither can he.

So we drove. Through the city with its brown fringes of early morning smoke, sleeping in its unnatural peace, along the Liffey, out by the Strawberry Beds, Chapelizod, Leixlip, Lucan. We halted by the canal gate at Kilcock to give him breakfast. Rose laid out a linen by the green canal bank, while I turned the car so he could face us. I opened the door, sat on the running-board by the front seat and wondered could he appreciate the picture she made: the white linen cloth on the green, the roses around her waist and behind her head the falling waters of the break. I fed him a sandwich, brushed the crumbs from his lapels and saw his blue eyes staring at a point behind her. A swan rose then, from the depths of the lock, an explosive snake of white. I saw his eyes follow it upwards till it got lost in the trees beyond.

The midlands shimmered in the midday sun, cattle stood motionless in the shade of trees; there seemed to be nobody about. The country slept in its cocoon, unchanged and unchangeable. Outside Athlone a wedding party passed us on a hayrick; near Ballinasloe a lorryful of soldiers trundled by. Rose hummed as I drove, snatches of melodies I knew from years of lessons, like an overture to her whole absent repertoire. I kept an eye on him in the back through the rearview mirror, his head jerking with each bump, his eyes turning with each new sight. We stopped at Kilreekill and finished the remains of Rose's sandwiches in the grounds of a gaunt limestone church. Then the light was falling, the evening sun slanted low over the Galway fields, silhouetting the jagged stone walls. We reached the Atlantic, set in swathes of limestone, and turned left along its coast through towns I'd heard him speak of: Kinvara, Ballyvaughan, Doonyvarden and when the light was fading, I stopped in the middle of what was like a stone desert. Why are you stopping? Rose asked. I want him to see it before the light goes, I told her. He campaigned here with De Valera in 1917.

I looked at him in the back seat, his face as gaunt as the stone walls that surrounded the stone fields, his beard the same limestone grey. If anything would suit his condition, I told her, it would be these fields: grey, immobile, furious and silent. As the light fell his profile seemed to glow with a light of its own; all distinction between him and the stones behind him slowly vanished. His breath rose and fell with hardly a murmur and then seemed to disappear. He was simply silent. I watched him in silence, then in a rash of sudden panic, reached out and touched his cheek. The beard quivered and the spell was broken. I drove on.   **155**

Lisdoonvarna announced itself from the brow of a hill, a string of sad-coloured lights below us like a circus which, when we drove down, we found to be a square, each lamppost strung with bulbs. I want to kiss you, Rose said suddenly. You can't, I said, not here. It's those bulbs, she said, they seem to lack the celebratory touch. Kiss him then, I said when the car had stopped, and she did. She leaned backwards in the car, planted a kiss on the cheek nearest to her. I saw his eyes flicker, but nothing else. He's stopped smiling, I said. Because I kissed him? she asked. No, I said. Something in the air . . .

We checked into the Spa Hotel, a mildewed affair with a lounge with an odour of stale Guinness. A glass-panelled veranda looked out on the square. A smattering of small farmers sat there, two women with spinsterish spectacles, a maid dressed in widow's black. I wheeled Father through to the reception.

For the waters? the concierge asked, part sympathy and all inquisition.

Yes, I said, they come well recommended.

Work wonders with the joints, she said; lumbago, arthritis, what have you. But don't expect miracles.

I don't, I said. I wanted to sign, but she was unstoppable.

If it's miracles you want, she said, here's your man. She tapped the wall behind her.

Who's your man? I asked her.

Sylvester Quirk, she told me, seventh son of a seventh son. Hands that could make a dead man walk. Find him every day on the road to O'Brien's Tower on the cliffs.

She pushed the book towards me and I signed. She kept on, about illnesses cured, bones made straight, tumours that vanished into thin air. She took two bulky keys then from a row of them next to the sign advertising the healer. She led us down a low corridor to two adjacent rooms overlooking a small back yard. You'd have trouble with the stairs, she said, and opened one room, then the next. Breakfast from eight to ten, she said, lunch at midday and your evening meal whenever you fancy. Rose thanked her and dispatched her with a glance.

I wheeled Father in, to the damp yellow walls, the single bed and the gas-jet set in the fireplace. Somewhere outside a dog barked.

While Rose and he rested I walked around the square. The coloured lights swung gently from their posts and beneath one of them, in the greenish wash the bulbs gave to their environs, was a figure with a bicycle. Collar upturned, a cloud of cigarette smoke above him like a halo of green. I recognised the smallest of the three, Oliver. Where's your companion? I asked him, when I had crossed to his side. Don't you worry your sweet head about him, he said. Tomorrow night, high tide, the beach at Spanish Point. You'll be there. If you insist, I told him. Damn right I do, he said.

We took him to the springs next morning, a low-roofed collection of huts over a bubbling pool. He drank the sulphurous water obediently and then I undressed him, lifted him with a male nurse into the bath of carved rock. The water bubbled round him, grey-coloured, insipid, and he suffered it in his usual silence, eyes staring at me with an expression of anguished surprise. When his time was up we lifted him, wrapped him in a white towel and sat him back in his chair to dry.

157

Will it work? Rose asked me when I had him clothed and wheeled him out once more.

Who knows, I said. We made it to the square, both thinking the same thought.

That boy, she said.

The one at Spanish Point? I said.

Yes, she said.

Do you really believe, I asked her, that something will happen?

It's not a matter of that, she said. It's something in the air.

What? I asked her.

Hope, she said.

I convinced myself to believe her. We winched him into the back seat once more and drove. The road seemed to lead us with a sense of inevitability, the low stone walls, the bent blackthorns, the fields of limestone now interspersed with green. We had asked no directions, but somehow I knew that I would know the spot when I found it. The sun came through the clouds and raked a low silver light which obscured the corners. But I turned one corner and there it was.

A withered tree with coins hammered into the bark, medals strung from them, faded pictures of the Virgin and in place of leaves, a mass of ribbons tied up and down the dead branches. They shivered in the morning breeze. Two walls led from the tree to a rough stone grotto. The walls were lined with crutches, blackthorn sticks, old orthopaedic boots, a crushed and rotten wooden wheelchair. A woman in black sat in a chair at the grotto entrance knitting.

158   I drew the car to a halt by the tree. There was the sense

of death about the place. Do you feel it, Rose? I asked. She said nothing, drew in her breath. The woman in black raised one arm and beckoned. I'm afraid, Rose, I said. Of what? she asked. Her lips were tight with a suppressed excitement. The woman beckoned again. I'm afraid it might be true, I told her. You can't be, she said. The woman beckoned a third time. I opened the door, walked out.

The ribbons fluttered in the breeze and there was a soft tinkle. I saw a silver bell, hanging from one of the dead branches. I walked forwards on the limestone slabs that led to the grotto and overturned a wooden crutch. It clattered off the stone. I bent to pick it up and the woman smiled, quite toothless.

You'll want the boy, she said. I nodded. For yourself? she asked. My father, I said, and she smiled again. Her needles clattered softly all the time. Bring him up then, she said. I waited for her to say something else but she returned to her needles as if I had vanished from her world. I walked backwards then, one step at a time. I looked from her to Rose in the car. Rose gestured with her hand.

I opened the door and sat beside her. Do you think this is wise? I asked.

Nothing is or has been wise, she said.

Is that a yes? I asked.

The woman gestured once more. There was an authority there which I could only obey. Come with me, Rose, I said. She nodded. I got out and opened her door, then opened his. She took one arm of the wheelchair, I took the other and together we eased him backwards until the rubber wheels bumped on the limestone slabs. I took his weight then, turned him and began to move towards the grotto, but felt Rose's hand on my shoulder.   **159**

Wait one minute, she whispered. She looked down at her hands, placed one finger and thumb over her wedding ring and drew it off. She reached up to the tree where a blue ribbon fluttered, and tied a knot round the ring.

What will that do? I asked her.

It's a sign, she said. If I could undo the past I would.

What bit would you change? I asked.

Whatever bit would help him, she said.

I looked at the ring, swinging idly against the grey sky. When the past overtakes the present, I wondered, what tense does it form? Then I turned and pushed him towards the grotto. The woman was back at her needles, unconcerned with us now that it had been decided. The long skein of some garment hung between her knees, below which was a copper bowl, coins and crumpled notes sitting in it. How much? I asked her. Whatever the gentleman thinks, she said. I pulled the roll I had been given by Soames from my pocket and peeled off ten notes. God be with you, sir, she said, her head still bent down, showing us the combed and glittering plane of her scalp.

I pushed him towards the stone entrance, shaped like a rough horseshoe. I could hear the regular dripping of water from inside, together with the low murmur of an adolescent voice. There was a slight incline, where his wheelchair took on its own momentum and pulled me suddenly inside. There was darkness then, the smell of funereal damp and stagnant water. I could feel Rose's arm at my elbow. Then gradually the gloom lifted, as my eyes grew accustomed to it. I could see a boy, sitting on a rock by a pool of water, a woman bent before him, her blouse pulled up to reveal her curved back. The boy, dressed in a suit like a diminutive cattle-salesman, dipped a thin white hand in the water and passed it over her back repeatedly, as he murmured to himself. The words were unrecognisable, came out of his lips with a whispered tension, like a murmur of pain. Then he pulled her blouse down and raised two dull eyes in our direction.

The woman raised herself stiffly, apologetically, as if embarrassed to be seen like this, and edged past us, her head and torso bent to one side. I stood there, waiting for the boy to acknowledge us, then looked at his unresponsive eyes and realised he was blind. I heard a voice from outside.

Go to him, he knows what ails you, she said, to the rhythm of her clacking needles.

The boy sat still, his head cocked to one side, listening to the wheels approach. He stretched out one hand, which came to rest neatly on Father's head. The thin fingers traced the mane of hair down to the forehead, then over his nose and lips, as if drawing his profile with an invisible pen. I saw Father's eyes flicker, then the lids fall slowly over them as if into a sleep. Bring him closer, the boy said, in a voice that was rural and matter-of-fact. I obeyed, pushing the chair to the edge of the pool. The boy's hand took up his chin again and traced the same line down his chest. The fingers began opening the buttons of his shirt, with an extraordinarily rapidity. The other hand reached down to the pool, came up cupped with water which he dabbed over the white hairs of Father's sunken chest. Then the hand reached up to his head again and pushed it downwards, like a pliant doll, so his forehead touched his knees. One hand pulled up his jacket and shirt, exposing the white knuckles of his spine, while the other dipped once more in the pool, raising to let the water run in rivulets

161

down the exposed skin. The murmuring began then, as if he had found what he wanted, his thin lips quivering with the half-words that escaped them. I turned and could see Rose, framed in the light by the ragged horseshoe of the entrance. The boy dipped, rubbed and murmured, so many times that the process became hypnotic, I lost count. Then the murmuring stopped; there was just the repetitive dripping water. The boy righted Father's clothing and stood. He edged his way around the wheelchair, reached two hands down to my father's fallen chin and whipped it upwards. There was a crack of twisting bone as Father's huge frame sat up, like an obedient doll. Don't worry, the boy whispered, it can't hurt him. He took his place back by the stone, rocking slightly backwards and forwards, his sightless eyes now somewhere else.

I drew Father backwards up the small incline, then wheeled him out to face the light. What do you think? I asked Rose, and she threw her eyes down to the woman, saying nothing. What do you think, Father? I asked as I reached the tree. He was as removed as ever, more so, if that were possible, his blue-veined lids covering his eyes. I reached up to the wizened tree and untied the ring from the ribbon where Rose had left it. Here, I told her, he would have wanted you to keep it.

We drove back through the barren landscape, fields of dead rock on either side. We were both quiet, as there seemed little to say. The rumble of the car, the occasional squawk of a passing crow served to accentuate the silence. As the road unravelled towards me I could imagine that silence stretching as far as the eye could see, over the moonscape of the Burren and beyond, over the quiet ocean to my left, the mackerel skies above us that embraced the whole island. We were in the country of silence, I realised, and any speech would only serve to remind us of it. I looked at Rose beside me and her face seemed older than I'd ever known it. I looked at him in the rearview mirror, as quiet as a rock, his chin settled on his chest, his eyes still closed. I could see a car behind him in the mirror, keeping a steady distance of a hundred yards or so, and knew we were being followed. When I reached Lisdoonvarna and wheeled around the square with its necklace of coloured bulbs the car drew to a halt on the other side. I parked opposite the Spa Hotel and looked at the wide-brimmed hats of the figures inside it. I saw a cloud of cigarette smoke obscuring the windscreen and recognised the G-men from the Castle.

Who are they? Rose asked as we moved him towards the hotel doors.

Who are who? I replied.

I saw you looking. The exchange of glances. Tell me.

I said nothing as we moved through the foyer, but inside the rooms she asked again.

We're here for something else, she said. Tell me what it is.

I looked at the square in the fading light outside and saw the car move off.

That business with the letters, I said.

What about it?

So I told her. As she listened she seemed to fall into a silence even deeper than my father's.

So it could never have worked, she said.

Why not?

Because you came down here for quite a different reason.

163

I could say nothing so she said nothing in reply. The three of us sat there in absolute stillness as the daylight paled and the coloured bulbs came up in the square outside.

I have to go now, Rose, I said.

Go on, she said. But take him with you.

Why? I asked her.

I can't stand it any more, she said.

So I drove with him to Spanish Point. The sky grew slowly into a magenta pall above us. The fields of stone gave way gradually to clutches of grass and then the sea came into view, stretching to the horizon under a full moon. The town when I reached it was as Soames had described it, a one-street promenade above a lengthy beach with a nuns' hostel perched on the north end, high above the water. I drove slowly down the road above the beach until the town was lost from view. I quietened the engine and eased him out of his perch in the back seat, bumped him down a series of broken steps onto the hard sand.

Another beach, Father, I said, but his eyes had fallen into their old silence, full of fury and surprise. And another sea, I said. The Atlantic this time. The wheels sank in the soft sand so I moved him out to the water's edge, where his chair bumped over the hard ridges. Can you imagine what our lines would catch here.

His head shuddered with barely perceptible jerks as I walked, as if he was nodding in reply. Maybe tonight, I told him, will have its moments. Maybe these are the hours towards which all the other hours pointed. Then I saw three figures down at the sea's edge, half hidden by an escarpment of rock, and suddenly wished Rose was with me.

164   Who will care for you, I asked him, when I'm gone?

They were clustered round a small boat: Oliver, the small one, Festy, the tall one, and the brooding Red.

What's with the old geezer? Red said when I drew near.

My father, I said; he's taking the waters.

What waters?

The waters in the sulphur springs, behind the Spa Hotel. If there's any bother, he's on his own, he said.

We stood then, watching the fading line of the horizon. I settled him there, facing the sea, and saw his eyes were open. The same cornflower blue, rimmed with reddened lids, they searched the ocean with the intensity of those around us. He shivered then, and I wondered for a moment was it the cold, or the awakening from the long sleep. Could that boy's magic work? I thought, then banished the thought as quickly.

Look, someone said.

Where? I asked.

What did you say? said Festy.

You said look, I said.

No I didn't, he spat back.

Then I looked down and saw my father's gaze riveted to a spot on the horizon.

The old geezer said it, Red muttered.

He couldn't. He can't speak.

Shut up and look, said Oliver. Over there.

There was a churning in the water, as if some leviathan was rising.

A dolphin, the same voice said.

That's no fuckin' dolphin, Festy shouted. It's your man—

I stared at Father's face. The eyes riveted to the spot, the same utter rigour.

Who said dolphin? I asked.

Would you shut up about your dolphins, Festy muttered. Look at that creature—

I could see the waters foaming, as if under great pressure from below. The turret came up first, then the sleek black hull, the waters falling away from it like skin off a bone.

I looked from him to the emerging monster and back again. His lips quivered, as if on the threshold of speech.

It's a submarine, Father, I said. Say it. A submarine.

The lips trembled, but no sound came out.

I am imagining things, I thought, making the dumb speak. I turned back to the sea and watched the monster make its full entrance. It rose slowly to the surface, the only turbulence in an otherwise quiet sea. I saw the turret open and a blond-haired figure emerge. I recognised Hans. He waved, over an acre of ocean. I waved back. You poor fucker, I thought. I have made you pay. He was shouting something. Irish, he said, Irish—and I couldn't distinguish the rest.

That's him? asked Red.

Yes, I said.

That's Rhett? You're sure?

Hans. I said. His name's Hans.

Come on, he said, pushing the boat towards the water.

I can't leave him here.

He'll be fine. And you'll do what you came here to do—

As the two brothers rowed I watched his diminishing figure in the wheelchair, immobile by the water's edge, eyes staring at me, almost pleading, as if I was leaving him for ever. What if the tide comes in? I shouted, in a sudden

panic.

It's on the turn, said Red, and whipped me round. Now look at him, make sure it's him.

The conning tower loomed above us, like a cliff wall. I could see him up there waving, a sailor's holdall in his hand. Then he jumped. He hit the water about fifteen feet away and the brothers rowed towards him, as the vessel above us began to diminish, sink beneath the waves once more, throwing the waters into a fury. He grabbed the side of the boat then and pulled himself in, his blond hair plastered to his skull. Get out of here, Irish, he said, quick, it leaves a whirlpool. The brothers rowed again, furiously, back the way we had come. The wash the vessel left bobbed the boat around like a cork, and then it was gone and there was something like calm once more. Your country, he said. Yes, I told him. Your waters, he said. Yes, I said again. And your countrymen, he said, turning to the others.

Then I heard the outboard motors. First one from the east, another from the west, two more from somewhere near the shore.

What the fuck—said Red, and I turned and grabbed the German, flung us both overboard.

You fucking quisling, Red bellowed, and pulled a gun and began to fire into the water. I pulled Hans beneath, dragged him underwater towards the back of the boat.

Down there it was all peace. The white tail of the boat curved above us, the water dotted with puffs where the bullets struck. His face screamed at me silently and he struggled in my arms. I drew back and struck out at him but not hard enough for he wrenched himself free. I grabbed his legs as he swam upwards but couldn't hold him and we both gasped to the surface once more.   **167**

What is this! he screamed, spitting out water.

I could now see the military caps on the other boats in the moonlight, the barrels of the .303s held by the soldiers.

I'm delivering you, I said, into safer hands.

You have betrayed me—

Yes, I said, you could put it that way. I saw Red, towering above us with the gun, and suddenly the ocean was ablaze with light, blinding him, wrapping him in white like an angel. He dropped the gun, raised his arms tentatively. There was a searchlight on each vessel, bearing towards us, and one low fast boat came by and threw us a lifebuoy on a rope.

Why? spluttered Hans, clinging to it, the wash of the boats cresting over him.

Because, I said, there was no alternative. There's a camp in the Curragh, they'll take you there.

You broke your word, he said.

We're a neutral country, I said. I could never have helped you. I slipped from the buoy and came up again, coughing water. Your war's obscene—

I have my honour, he yelled.

Thank God one of us has, I said.

The boats were all around us, the noise of the engines deafening. Someone called in a thick country accent from a loudhailer. I looked up, saw Red with his arms raised and saw the smaller brother bring his oar down towards me. I tried to duck, but he caught me on the forehead and the world went thankfully dark.

I came to consciousness on the hard wet sand of the beach **168** some time later. A youth in a Local Defense Force uniform was bending over me, bringing a bowl of hot soup to my lips. What happened? I asked him.

They caught them, he said, fished them out of the water like drowned rats. There's an ambulance coming for you.

I don't need it, I said, rising.

There were soldiers up and down the strand, distant shouts to the search-lit boats out on the ocean. I staggered through the darkness; the moon had gone, the beach was one long shadow. Father, I called, trying to find my way to where I had left him. One soldier grabbed me by the arm. We're closing off the beach, he said.

I've to find my father, I said, in a wheelchair, by the promenade end.

Yes, he said, we found a wheelchair.

Not the wheelchair, I said, the man inside it. I felt ice in my stomach suddenly. Where, I asked him, where did you find it? He led me then, by torchlight, to the spot where I'd left him and I saw the chair, sitting wheel-deep in the water, quite empty. The tide had come in.

Where is he? I asked the soldier.

Where is who? he asked me back.

My father, I said. I left him sitting there.

That's all we found, sir, he said.

We searched all night—the beach, the dunes, the town above it—but found nothing. When the dawn came we turned the search to the sea itself but the tides there were such they would have drawn any object in it out with them. By noon they told me that to continue would be pointless.

I drove back then to Lisdoonvarna and found Rose pacing the square, filled now with camouflaged lorries and boys in ill-fitting military uniforms. Her face had the grey pallor that told me she already knew.

Is it true? she asked me, and I told her it was.

He must have walked, I said, through the water, out to sea.

You know he couldn't, she said.

I told her then about the voice that seemed to come from nowhere, could only have come from him. Maybe the boy did what he was paid for.

It makes no sense, she said. If he could walk, why walk into the sea?

Because he knew, I thought. So I said Yes, it makes no sense, he couldn't have walked.

We stayed three more weeks. Thinking a corpse might be washed up at the foot of the Cliffs of Moher, any point on the coastline from Galway to the Shannon. We took boats out daily, more for the comfort of doing something than in the hope that we would find him. A silence settled between us that we knew was permanent. At night I dreamt of him, traversing the waves of the Clare coastline like a merman, in an element that perhaps would have suited him more than most. Rose slept beside me, frozen in her loss, her body stiff and unattainable. Now that he was gone he was all she could desire, and I was the cause of the absence that gnawed at her, as she was of the absence that gnawed at me.

We ate silent breakfasts, surrounded by small farmers and their intended sweethearts, who came there for honeymoons, matches and cures for arthritis. We went as far as Aran one afternoon, and there, on a grey slab of island in the Atlantic, we admitted it was finished. The search for him, and for each other. The Clare coastline was a dull blur, a mist sheeted down from the west, she said little but That's it then. And it was, I agreed.

She took a train up to Sligo, to the mythical household she had filled me with years before. I had the urge to ask her could I see it, just once, but on the dull grey platform, waiting for the train, I knew it was useless. Goodbye, Donal, she said, and she kissed me. I'll be in touch about the house. And the train bore her off, through the scented hedgerows of the single-track line of the West Clare railway.

I drove home with only the wheelchair for company. I watched it in the rearview mirror, the country roads unwinding behind it. It was silent, and perfect, in a way, a memento of him, with the same quiet dignity I had found in him since I had come back. When I reached Bray, I found the boy had maintained the boats in perfect order.

We spent the rest of the Emergency fishing, which seemed as good a way as any of passing the conflagration. I sent Rose money when I could, played the piano at nights and tried to think of him as little as possible. Some days, under the sheets of rain, dragging herring out by the Kish I would look at the catch, see the dark shape of a porbeagle or dolphin among the slapping silver and imagine for a moment that I had caught him, his body having made the long journey home, the way salmon do. Some nights I would wake, look at the wheelchair gleaming in the moonlight by its spot at the window and think for a moment he had returned, was sitting there, silent, patient, inscrutable.

The news from Europe passed us by, seemed monstrous,

but somehow less intimate than the monstrosities we had accomplished. Rose came down from Sligo around the time of the siege of Stalingrad and we walked the promenade for an hour, before she collected her things. She had felt ill for weeks on her return, she told me, had feared she was pregnant, then discovered she wasn't and instantly regretted it. She was a widow now, she said, and in the country that had a certain status. We were both regretful, but empty of tears as she emptied her room. The dress I had bought her was packed neatly with the others, the ring was still on her finger. You could live here, I told her, if it took your fancy, but she shook her head and I understood why. So we said goodbye once more, by the Bray station this time, and I saw her borne off by the double track of the Great Southern Railway.

IV

Then, on the day after De Valera presented his condolences to the German embassy on the death of Hitler, I resurrected my father.

He had died in that other sea, to the west, and this smaller one outside my window, that I fished when the light was good, seemed to hold his spirit in a more companionable form. Rose was by now a memory, a bittersweet one, that scent of dried flowers matching the printed flowers on her dress, her upright back by the upright piano, her long blonde hair shifting as she played. I drank too much most nights, whiskey in the empty study and, when the night was clear and the humour took me, Guinness in the waterfron bars down near the Head. I would wake with the first light, walk out behind the house to where the Dargle river spilt into the harbour.

That river was a small insignificant one, almost an after- **173** thought to the layers of sand and silt that clogged its banks, but in the early morning when it reflected the sky it had a certain muddy poetry to it. I had clear memories of a king-fisher, scudding across the brown surface with its flash of royal blue, of the mullet that would hang beneath the bridge where the sewer pipe came out. I would sit beneath the huge metal girders of the railway bridge, watch these mullet and think of how the fish we had always caught together were of the unprepossessing kind: mullet, plaice, sole, an eel or two, the lazy kind, addicted to the grosser forms of waste, fun for catching, maybe, but not for eating. I would watch the somnolent arcs these mullet made, then hear the six-thirty from Cork to Dublin whacking by, shaking the earth I sat on, the huge metal girders, adding a ghostly ripple to the swatches of water, sending the mullet off in whip-like flashes to the darker corners that fish go to whenever they go.

My memories of him were dimming. The alcohol of each night didn't help, but I would substitute them with fancies. See him beneath the water, the fish we caught when we were younger draped round his neck in a tangle of eel, catgut, gill and reddened mouth for all the world like a wreath. Or smaller ones around his forehead like a halo, woven together like sprigs of myrtle, his head ascend-ing through them to a bowl of light which halates it in turn. Cleaving through the water upwards, in a dive re-versed, the white cloud and the blue sky reflected in the metal surface of the Dargle water and the angels, if they deigned to grace my fancy, rising with him, whipping this way and that in the stiff morning breezes. Then at times I would think of the banks of silt around the river conserv-ing his flesh, that dull sand we all return to and the rust-

174

coloured water holding whatever water inhabited him, spreading, the colour of old blood, out to those cold white horses that played on the sea beyond the river's mouth. His soul playing over it like that unseen wind that only showed itself on the water when it rippled, then shuddered as the train went by, that wind becoming a secondary gust the train sucked into itself, then dispersed among those frothy horses along the shore farther down the line.

These were fancies, easy to imagine with the warped clarity that too much whiskey brings. What proved impossible to imagine was what common sense told me—that he simply was no more. And the fact that the old prosaic reality proved impossible to picture while any alternative to it was blissfully simple proved something else to me in turn: that these layers of silt, those ovals of pig-iron above it, the six-thirty roaring to Dublin, Dublin itself and the sea beyond it served simply as an adjunct to his story. He died in the sea to the west and the sea itself depended on him for its continued existence, since why else would I have sat beside it, or beside this river, its drab, half-forgotten tributary? And to return to fish—for somehow fish are central to his tale—only seriously there when caught, dead, gutted and eaten, otherwise as elusive as memory itself, backwards flips on the surface of the water, shadows running to shadows. Fish were important in more ways than one. As the garland to our cruellest moments, and to our kindest ones and as a conduit to a whole river, even a sea of memories. The memory of those piscine armfuls led to other recollections which would ripple on the surface of my quotidian dreaming and drag me down with them. There was another sea there, but I was underneath it, the brown waters were as cold as dreaming is, and a cod or a ling or at times a codling would weave towards me and beyond with a memory pinned to it like a Fisheries Board tag. The sea was all about death, and death drew into itself all the moments of its attendant lives and my attempt to understand this sea had taken years now and one memory would draw me towards it, always the same, lapping like a rising tide when you had forgotten there was such a thing as water, for you had thought the tide had retreated, your bare feet had grown used to the hard scalloped sand and yet there it was, creeping round your ankles saying, in so many words, Remember me. And the memory was this. The two of us, laying nightlines for the umpteenth time at low tide.

I had travelled to the Curragh to visit Hans in the low collection of Nissen huts that constituted his prison. A plain of flat green as far as the eye could see dotted with clumps of grazing sheep, a copse of trees barely hiding the military barracks. He emerged from a group of half-starved Republicans, the grey pallor of his face now echoing the grey of his tattered uniform. You have betrayed me, Irish, he said.

Yes, I said, betrayal seems to be my destiny. And what does this say of these times where betrayal becomes the only viable response?

He didn't answer, so I proffered him the brown paper parcel I held which contained a bottle of Irish whiskey and two strings of fine black pudding. He hesitated, as if the last vestiges of his pride were reviving themselves, then stretched out his hands and pulled it towards him.

Schnapps, he said, as he ripped open the paper, couldn't you have brought me schnapps? Though he pulled the cork from the whiskey and began to drink it anyway.

176   At least you won't be shot here, I told him.

True, he said, you have other more refined means of torture.

What are they? I asked, and he told me how they heard Mass each morning, played hurling and handball each afternoon and studied Irish at night.

You should join the classes, I told him, you might learn something.

Linguistics, he said, was never my strong point.

Then I remembered his mathematical leanings, and told him how his mentor Heisenberg had been captured during the Rhine advance and was being held incommunicado outside London.

He will understand the true nature of uncertainty, then, he said. He passed me the bottle and I drank and after a time his eyes lost their resistance. Maybe I'll stay here, Irish, he said.

You have no alternative, I said, looking at the rolls of barbed wire across the fields behind him.

No, he said, when the whole thing is over, and it will be over soon, yes?

Soon, I assured him.

I will learn your language and your violent sports and teach mathematics in a boys' school. Your president is mathematical? he asked.

He runs the country on Euclidean principles, I told him.

Maybe I could help him then, Hans said, the whiskey making him dewy-eyed. It would be good for once, to be of use. And Irish, he said, as I made to go. Just so you know. I cannot blame you. In your situation, who knows, I would have done the same.

That evening in the Railway Bar I learnt that his Führer had immolated himself and that De Valera had, with all the logic of Zeno, presented himself at the diplomatic offices of the Reich to offer his condolences. The conversation in the bar ranged from the supportive to the censorious. Backing a loser there, said a local landscape gardener, sucking heavily on a cigarette. Sure what has he been backing since the whole bother began, said a coal merchant whose two sons served in the Irish Guards, his blackened hands clutching a half-empty pint. If it's not one shower, he muttered cryptically, it's the other.

I drank and listened and felt the same dull ache. Some facts draw all other facts into themselves, create a mystical union between disparate things, and the thought of De Valera brought me back once more to him, to his study with the green baize table and his fingers pasting newspaper cut-outs of Civil War atrocities into the ledger he kept for that purpose.

I finished my drink and edged my way outside, hoping to be rid of that memory. But out there the moon was full and illuminated perfectly the green swath that led to his house, etched each small gazebo on the seafront in a child-like blue. I walked across the grass, which was wet with May dew, to the promenade. The tide was out and the moonlight touched each ridge on the empty sand and blurred the distances, so that sand was all there was to the horizon, where the thinnest line of silver intimated the sea. I knew the full moon was the cause of it, made the tides full and the absences fuller, and remembered my dream again, him running barefoot across the strand in advance of the crushing wave while the doctor ran to the house with his black bag and Maisie rubbed her hands on her smock on the prom with a distracted air.

I wanted to exorcise him then once and for all, put him

finally to rest, and went to the house, pulled open the door of the cupboard below the stairs and found the metal rods, rusting now, bent into a circle at the top with the old gut still tied to them. The lines had discoloured, turned green in places, amber in others and the old blunt hooks still hung from them. I wrapped them in one hand, took a coal shovel in the other, strode outside down the steps on to the sand and began to walk. I walked towards the line of silver that was the tide, but never found it. The closer I came, it seemed, the more it retreated. I saw a worm cast, dug out rapid spadefuls, chasing the source, and pulled out three rags. I walked on, but the tide came no closer, then dug again. I came up with some lugs this time, walked again until my effort to reach that sea seemed futile. It was the same thin line on the horizon of quiet silver, taunting me with its absence.

I have fallen out of time, I thought, where distances have lost all depth and this walk could continue for ever. I looked to my left and could see the Kish lighthouse prodding smugly forward from the silver line and looked back and saw the promenade with its painted townscape behind, farther than I'd ever seen it. I thought, this must be the place then, that magical place you will always take with you no matter how far and in what direction you walk. The moon was right above me on its meridian, if a moon can have one, and washed my form in light but left me shadowless. So I jammed each rod deep in the pristine sand, pulled the catgut tight and skewered a worm to each hook. I said a prayer for fish then, the kinds of fish he would have been proud of, and began my walk back. I turned after a time, half expecting the nightlines to be right behind, as if that spot would follow me no matter how far

I walked from it, but saw them standing, thirty yards or so away, silhouetted darker against the sand, the worms squirming gently in the moonlight. I knew their place was the right one then, the place where both worlds meet, and made my way back to the promenade and was surprised to find it not so far away after all.

I slept a quiet, dreamless sleep, the kind you remember from childhood in a blanket, it seemed, of peaceful blue. I woke to the sunlight flooding my window, not knowing what time it was, then heard the bells ringing for the first Mass. It was Sunday, I remembered, so I dressed and went downstairs and prepared the kind of breakfast we used to eat together. I made too much for one, absentmindedly, as if the appetites of Rose and him still prevailed in the kitchen. I was hungry, though, so I ate it all. The wedge of sunlight came through the window, illuminating the spot where his wheelchair sat, and served to remind me of the halo it once gave to the fringes of his beard. Then I wondered how the tides were and walked outside.

The sun was hidden by the empty bath-house at the end of the terrace. It spread a veil of soft rose light across the empty sands, over which the tide had come and gone. I walked from the shadows the terrace threw into the wash of pink across the scuffed grass and up the broken wall on to the promenade. I could see my nightline in the distance, the thin black cord sagging under the weight of seven flapping shapes, bending the rods inwards. I took my shoes off, walked in bare feet down the granite steps across the stones to the stretches of hard ribbed sand. I kept my eyes on those dark flapping shapes, half fearful that if I stopped looking they would disappear. I could make out the outlines of a plaice, two pollock, a bream, a dogfish and a salmon bass. Between them was a larger one, elemental, that I couldn't recognise. As I came closer it revealed itself, outsize and majestic, a hooked creature from some lower depths, shuddering occasionally in the morning breeze, quite silver-scaled, eyes bulging and distended, tulip-mouthed, on its forehead a curved and perfect horn. As it flapped, its gills shuddered with the last gasps of air. I bent down to touch it, wondering what it was, and heard a thin pale cry come from it, as it died in the unfamiliar light. I tried to place it, this outlandish shape silhouetted against the morning sun over the sea, when I saw something else emerge from the water behind it, from beyond the tulip mouth, from the line of lazily washing tide.

The trousers on this figure were rolled up around the calves, the bony, ancient feet splashing the water, the head bent down as if looking for periwinkles. Then he looked up and at me and walked forwards, the beard and the grey hair fringed by the sun behind him.

There were drops glistening like dew on his tweed suit, but the suit itself didn't seem wet. His forehead had the sheen of a film of sea water and his beard was peppered with the same beads of dew. He was carrying his shoes in his hand, like me, and looked younger and older at the same time. He stood on the other side of the line of fish. He looked at the fish, then at me, then at the fish again.

There was nothing to say. I'd fished him from the sea somehow, dragged him from one element to the other with an invisible line. He stood there blinking in the unfamiliar light, looking from the fish to his feet, up at me again. He was nothing like he had been, I could sense that immediately. He took one step towards me, then stopped, **181** the hooks touching his waistcoat, his eyes inchoate, his mouth serene. He was lost and yet found. I reached forwards, touched his real sleeve and felt the salt water there as I led him round the line. He looked at me apologetically as if he was late, many years late, then pulled the rods from the sand, gathered up the armfuls of fish and began to walk to the shore. They could have been the fish he had left there all those years ago, when he gave that strange cry and ran towards Maisie and the doctor on the promenade. His feet left prints in the sand, just as they had done in life. The dead must have weight then, I thought, and followed the prints, several steps behind him. He climbed the granite walkway and stood on the promenade among the first early-morning strollers, awkwardly, like a bird that was unused to land. I took his elbow, which was as light and brittle as a feather, and walked him towards the house. The rods dragged and the lines dripped water on the concrete beneath our feet. I led him from the stares of the passers-by to the railings and the sparse sea grass towards the terraces. He saw the door and stopped, as if the sight of it was painful to him, then started again as I moved him forwards, opened it and ushered him inside. We stood together in the darkened hallway as we had so many times before.

I felt guilty as always but a strange thrill ran through my fingers which was unfamiliar. Through the accident of fishing, I had brought him back, I knew, from whatever place he had inhabited. He stood now in the dark of the house staring at the light outside and all the harshness seemed gone from him, the silent fury. He was lost and malleable, and somehow more human than when he had lived. We have so much to say to each other, I thought, and wondered would we say any of it, then took the fish from his hands, closed the door with my foot and led him into the kitchen. The plates were on the table, with the breakfasts I had eaten, thoughtlessly as it turned out, since here he was and he could well be hungry.

Are you . . . , I asked, and didn't think to finish the question, but he must have divined it anyway since he nodded, vigorously. I took the fish from his arms and looked at the unfamiliar one. It seemed the most appetising of the lot, part skate, part sea-horse, so I cut it, gutted it and placed strips in the pan. It gradually began to sizzle, the flesh white, succulent and transparent, and a magical smell of burnt honey flooded the room. The scales on the horn fell off and the flesh began to brown, so I sliced it free of the rest, skewered it on a fork and handed it to him to eat. The flesh crumbled in his lips and he smiled, welcoming the taste, and handed the fork back to me. I ate it in turn and knew why he had smiled as the unfamiliar filled my mouth, flesh that was hardly flesh, fish that was no known fish, taste that was somewhere beyond the bounds of sensation. It was there, crumbled and was gone, leaving the aftertaste of honey.

He spoke then, as if the taste had released something. His voice was quiet, with none of the fury it had held in life. If the dust that wheeled in the sunlight that came through the window had made a sound, it would have sounded like his voice.

He told me he had been walking, and that he seemed to have been walking ever since he had last seen me. I had left him by that sea and it had surpassed all of my efforts to move him. The boy's hands achieved nothing, the water down his naked spine, the muttered words and prayers; **183**

nothing had moved him till he saw that expanse of dark blue. So he did what he had known he would always do, since I had left for that war I had wanted to partake in: he walked. And he headed for what seemed most natural, the ridges of sand under the fine woollen socks she had knitted for him, then the water creeping round his socks and meeting his ankles. He had looked up and down the strand, seen figures in the darkness, one of which no doubt was me, but he wanted to know me most of all the way he'd known me long ago, when we both would stand ankle-deep in the water all those years past, before my mother had died. I had no memory of her, he told me, which always troubled him, since an indigent figure, lying in a bed perpetually, should not be counted as a memory proper; and he had kept walking and those thin loins of his which had been dead all those years came to life again, life of a kind, of a new kind, and he had known then what he had to do. Which was to bury himself in that ocean, since speech between us had always been difficult, but there was another kind of speech which he now wanted. If he were to die, he told me, he would rather die in that element which had given voice to all we never said. It was our language, he knew that and suspected I had always known that, and the accidents that had muddied our efforts to be in that language were just that: accidents. The accident of her absence was the first, which led to a silence that was hard to break. So as he walked and the dark blue moved from his loins to his chest to the beard under his chin, he began to fill that silence and say all the things he had never said to me. And there were so many of those things it seemed the sea was hardly big enough to hold them, so when his feet
184   left the hard ridges of the sand and were treading on water

alone another kind of walking began. It was a simpler kind, walking through no known landscape, carrying on that conversation with me about the things we never talked about in life, for this was death, he was certain of that, this walk along no known surface with only the ocean of all that had happened above.

So this was the way the dead talked, I thought, watching him standing there, swaying slightly in the kitchen, the water beginning to dry in patches on his suit, eyes slightly distant and confused but with a smile I'd never seen before underneath his beard. They whisper, they create a silence that fills the whole room with another kind of speech, and if a noise was made by those particles of dust wheeling gently in the sunlight, this would be it. The sound of dust rubbing elbows, rubbed by sunlight. I reached for another strip of that unique fish from the sizzling pan and held it out to him. He took it and ate and began again. But began is the wrong word, since from the silence with no speech, there was simply silence and speech.

Rose, he told me, Rose had known the folly of it the moment I had left. He had married her for me, she had married him for me, but these follies take their own momentum. I must have known that, he said, from the follies of my own: they create their own accidental excitement and only later does one realise, it was not about that at all. But by then the folly is erect and fully built, filling the garden all on its own. The church on the windy hill where he had married my mother was not ready for a second visitation, but the dress I had refused to see, the preparations for the wedding breakfast I didn't attend, the ring he had bought her all had created such a frisson that it seemed to be about that after all.   **185**

Only when they came back to the cold living-room did they both realise the profound futility, how the reason for their union had been driven away by the fact of it and how that reason had been me. They had looked at the empty piano and after an age of the same silence he had asked her to play and when she shook her head, the blonde tresses, for she had done them in ringlets for the occasion, moving from one side to the other, he had known the precise and absolute folly of it. But one lives, and I of all people must have known that, one makes the best of it and in their case they did until they heard the news of where I had gone. Walking—he seemed to have been walking for ever—by the promenade, looking down on the same sea that I had drawn him out of, he was hit by the folly one last time and felt his ribcage burst. He grabbed the railings and remembered leaving me by the hooks fifteen years before when he had seen the doctor running. He grabbed the railings, but the railings hadn't held him and he fell backwards. And she had found him there like a beetle, all four limbs in the air, all of them useless. She had carried him back with the help of Vance the chemist who was passing and then learnt a kind of love, he supposed, as she wheeled him from room to room of the house that was all emptiness. For there was a fondness there, he told me, that could have blossomed into a union but the fact of the wheelchair had saved them from all that. She would read the newspapers to him daily then, never knowing whether he heard or not, and he had come to welcome his trapped state, the inertia that had become his lot; he took comfort in the patterns of sun across the linoleum floor and the dust that circled round in it, since the

news she read to him was barbaric, unthinkable, so much so

that silence was blessed. Then one day I was suddenly there again.

He stopped and stared at the same patterns of sun on the same floor. I reached for the pan to take another strip of fish and was surprised at how much flesh the fish contained. I ate a strip, tasted the same honey and handed one to him.

The fish would never diminish, he told me, it would provide its meat until everything was said. We were there in a continual present, until there were no mysteries left. Then he could go back to that greater mystery. He was never one for talking, he told me, ironic really since that was part of the trouble: the words that would have cleared the muddle never sprang to his lips. He had always hoped silence would do the trick, an unspoken understanding, and if all else failed there was always fishing. He could see the thing he was then, in his tweed suit, his son beside him at the living-room table, Maisie serving us both, how inadequate it must have been, and realise how much of it was accidental. We are born out of accidence, he told me, and out of accidence we imagine is created the necessary, the indomitable self, which, if we only knew it, could change in a minute with our intervention. But we fill our years, he told me, with the business of that self, with the way it walks down the promenade, takes the black car to work, the way it sits at the green baize table, fills the world with what it thinks is purpose, till the range of possibilities has narrowed to the ones just that self wants. And death, he told me, is the realisation of all those lost possibilities in the life we have left. You see each of them as you walk, you see how if any one of them had been grasped, things could have been different.

He had seen me walk down the promenade, he told me, the day I came back, sitting by the green baize table where she would leave him on odd days, my gait and the holdall I had carried like a sailor's, and had willed with every piece of himself to be able to move when I walked into that room, but the more he willed, it seemed, the more the rigour took hold of him. He had heard my knock on the door, Rose's voice and mine, then my feet ascending the stairs and listened, unable to turn as I mentioned his name. He had welcomed every moment of our walks along that promenade, accepted the simple pleasure of listening and realised his condition somehow gave me voice. He had wondered whether if he could have answered would I have spoken so much.

He had known the inevitability of what would follow from the moment I came back. If he could have said, please don't worry, he would have, but even that was denied him. His only terror was that guilt on my part would lead back into silence. And when that happened and my silence came, a rage would come on him in waves: rage at the old muddle once more, since if he couldn't talk, all he would have wanted was for me to, and the rage gave him movement one morning and he wrote on the sugar but the worry eluded him. And he came to realise that even that would be misunderstood. So all our efforts to revive him he concurred in; he would have walked if he could if only to say that, clearly and unambiguously so we would have understood. But he came to see then that even Rose was not what it was about. Rose was excluded in turn from this raging need between us, the coming together and away, the speech, the muddle and the further silences. So when that sea presented itself to him with its submarine like a child's toy in a bath and he found at last he could walk, that was the way he had walked. It was our element, after all. And he had walked thus since, in a wash of the past till one day as he walked he saw light above him, playing round him in shafts, and realised he could surface again. And coming to the surface, he had seen me there, playing with the lines as if I had never stopped in two decades. And he realised those lost possibilities were not losses, they were always there, intimated by the fabric of what had come to happen: unravel one of them and the infinity of others present themselves. And that was the sum of what was. And he nodded at the pan and said we had come to the end of that fish.

All the water had dried from his suit and it seemed to be collecting dust as he sat there. A pale sheen of it covered his cheek and his beard. He turned to the window and scattered wafts of it, like gold dust. I saw the reddish hue in the room and realised the day had gone its course while we spoke and it was approaching evening. You know, he said, the tide should be far enough out now for a nightline. And he turned and walked through to the hallway and I heard the old clattering down below the stairs as he gathered the rods. Are you ready? he asked, and I nodded and followed him out to the sparse sea grass. We climbed the broken wall and walked along the promenade towards the stone steps. The sun was behind us, throwing long shafts over the grass, the concrete walkway and the beach beyond. I heard the five-thirty go by for Dublin and felt the tremor in the earth and followed him down the steps to the sand. I took my shoes off, as did he, when the hard ridges began with

189

the water between them. He dug with the spade while I pulled the worms through the wet, crumbling sand, squirming, as if they knew what faced them. We untangled the line then, jammed the rods down and skewered a worm to each hook. And it was then, with the worms swinging once more in the evening air, that he chose to depart. He walked towards the sea, trousers rolled around his calves, and I noticed a pale moon against the blue beyond. He walked quietly, as if I had never existed, as if no conversation had ever begun. I sat on the sand and the skewered worms dangled in front of my eyes, his figure way beyond them, just a silhouette now. My eye travelled down the line of worms, to see where he was headed. And it was then I noticed a figure pacing with calm expectancy, way beyond, at the lip of the water. A pair of high heels, incongruous on the sand, a blue Edwardian dress and a straw hat. What seemed like a bag, clasped with both hands by her stomach. My only memory of her had been sitting in the bed upstairs, coughing. I saw his thin stick-like silhouette walk towards her, neither disappointed nor surprised, take her arm and walk, like a couple on a last stroll on a ravishing summer's evening. I knew that she, of all things, was what he most wanted. I saw them walk then, in the thin evening light, across planes of sand, sea and air, mauve, purple and silver, till the light became so thin they could be seen no longer.

I looked down at my bare feet and saw he had taken his shoes.

GLOSSARY

Black and Tans

The auxiliary police force that the British hurriedly sent to Ireland in 1918 and 1919 as replacements for the domestic Irish constabulary, which almost unanimously resigned in protest after hostilities with the British broke out. The name comes from the improvised nature of their uniforms.

Civil War

In 1921 the British government opened talks with the separatists. A treaty was signed and ratified in December 1921, though the Republican faction, led by Eamon De Valera, denounced such concessions as the exclusion of Northern Ireland from the Irish Free State and the imposition of an oath of allegiance to the British Crown. The Free Staters, led by Michael Collins, argued that under the circumstances the concessions were acceptable. The Irish parliament narrowly ratified the treaty in January 1922 after the stormy Treaty Debates. When the general elections of June 1922 gave the Free Staters a majority, the Republicans boycotted parliament. A full-scale civil war broke out and lasted until the middle of the fall, when the balance tilted to the Free State government. With British approval, the government ratified a national constitution in December 1922.

Michael Collins

The hero of the War of Independence (the Anglo-Irish War) of 1918–21, in which he rose to command all Irish rebel forces, Collins became the head of the provisional government of the Irish Free State in January 1922. He assumed military command of the Free Staters in the Civil War and was killed in a Republican ambush on August 22, 1922.

W. T. Cosgrave

The Taoiseach (*Tee*-shock), or prime minister, of the Irish Free State from 1922 to 1932, Cosgrave galvanized the disorganized and leaderless Free Staters into a workable government. In 1927 he passed legislation that forced the boycotting Republicans to participate in parliament.

The Dáil

Dáil is the Gaelic word for "assembly" and the official name of the Irish parliament.

Eamon De Valera

The American-born linguist, political theorist, and leader
of the Republican movement. Captured by the British in

the bloody Easter uprising of 1916, he was spared the death penalty because of his U.S. citizenship. After a spectacular breakout from a Welsh prison, he returned to Ireland, rejected the Anglo-Irish treaty as negotiated by Michael Collins, resigned as president of the parliament, and led the Republicans through the Civil War. He grudgingly acquiesced to W. T. Cosgrave's legislation in 1927 and reentered government. De Valera took the prime ministership in 1932 and held it almost continuously until his election as president of Ireland in 1959 and again in 1966.

The Free State
The Anglo-Irish treaty that created the Irish Free State produced a divided Ireland, with six of its thirty-two counties, all in the north, remaining in British possession, and the rest retaining the accouterments of British dominion. In the new Irish constitution of 1937—which created the titular position of president of Ireland—the name "Irish Free State" was officially replaced by the name "Eire."

Lord Haw-Haw
William Joyce, the Brooklyn-born, Irish- and English-educated Nazi collaborator who broadcast propaganda from Germany during much of World War II. He was executed by the British for treason in 1946 (unlike De Valera, his U.S. citizenship didn't spare him; he had illegally acquired a British passport in 1933, and prosecutors argued that this made him a British subject).

I.R.A.
The Irish Republican Army, the military arm of the Sinn Fein, the Irish independence movement.

Irregulars
Official term for those I.R.A. members who fought the Free Staters in the Civil War.

I.T.G.W.U.
The Irish Transport and General Workers' Union.

The Republican Movement
Those who politically and militarily supported the idea of Ireland's becoming a republic completely independent of the British empire.

The War of Independence
Also called the Anglo-Irish War of 1918–21. The guerrilla war conducted against the British in Ireland after Britain refused to grant Ireland independence as called for by the Home Rule Act of 1914.

The Truce
The cease-fire agreed upon by Britain and the Irish parliament in July 1921, when independence negotiations began.

The Treaty with Britain
The agreement, negotiated by Michael Collins, that recognized the partition of Ireland into North and South and granted imperial dominion status to the South.

ABOUT THE AUTHOR

Born in Ireland, NEIL JORDAN is an award-winning writer and internationally celebrated film director. He is the author of a collection of stories, *Night in Tunisia,* and two previous novels, *The Past* and *The Dream of a Beast.* His films include *Angel, The Company of Wolves, Mona Lisa* and *The Crying Game,* which won the Oscar for Best Screenplay in 1993. His latest film is *Interview with the Vampire.* He lives in Dublin.

ABOUT THE TYPE

This book was set in Bembo, a typeface based on an old-style Roman face that was used for Cardinal Bembo's tract *De Aetna* in 1495. Bembo was cut by Francisco Griffo in the early sixteenth century. The Lanston Monotype Machine Company of Philadelphia brought the well-proportioned letter forms of Bembo to the United States in the 1930s.